# JEANMARIE
## and the Runaways

# JEANMARIE
## and the Runaways

### APPLE VALLEY
### MYSTERIES

## Lucille Travis

Baker Books

A Division of Baker Book House Co
Grand Rapids, Michigan 49516

© 2000 by Lucille Travis

Published by Baker Books
a division of Baker Book House Company
P.O. Box 6287, Grand Rapids, MI 49516-6287

Printed in the United States of America

ISBN 0-8010-4470-7

Library of Congress Cataloging in Publication Data is on file at the Library of Congress, Washington, D.C.

Scripture quotation is from the King James Version of the Bible.

For current information about all releases from Baker Book House, visit our web site:
                    http://www.bakerbooks.com

# Contents

# ". . . and then we will escape."

Streaks of faint pink touched the sky just above the still shadowy trees at the edge of the labor camp. A boy sat up slowly. Throughout the camp men began preparing food for their morning meal. Near the boy a young girl slept on a straw mat on the ground. He let her sleep while he rolled up his own mat and tossed it into the back of the truck. From crude shelters tacked together with cardboard, wood, and newspaper other workers came to drink coffee and eat the meal of beans and bread.

The young girl, awake now, braided her long, black hair for the day. The boy had already heated water in an old tin pot. While she ate, the boy left to wash in the ditch at the edge of the camp. There was no clean water in the camp. The owners of the farm provided only the bare campground for the Mexicans who worked in their fields until the onions were picked and moved on. The boy hated the dark, smelly water in the ditch, but he had no choice. At night he heated the water they would use for drinking and cooking the next day. In the morning the creek must do for washing.

At the edge of the creek a fellow worker splashed his face, soaked a bandana to wear around his neck, and slicked back his hair. "Ay, this heat is the devil, no?" he said. The man did not wait for small talk but hurried away to eat. The boy did the same. They must be in the fields before the sun was fully risen. They would not return to the camp until dark.

The boy ate quickly, and the girl finished and went to the ditch. He watched her as she hurried. He was older, twelve, and even for him stooping all day among the endless rows of vegetables, hour after hour, dawn till nightfall, drained him of all strength. His back ached and his legs cramped after a full day's work. For the girl it was worse. She could not work so fast as he, and neither of them could keep up with the older workers, but it did not matter. Under the eyes of the crew leader no one dared to slacken his or her pace. At noon they would stop to eat, then return to work under the hot sun. There were no rests.

The boy listened as the crew leader gave orders. The leader took care of everything, including the money, and charged for everything. The boy too must pay for food and housing no matter how unfit it was. From the little earnings each worker had left, the crew leader took his share.

All morning, flies and strange insects the boy had no name for pestered him as he picked. In the next row he saw the girl brush away something. Sweat poured down into his eyes, and time and again he wiped it away with his shirt. His back ached from stooping. His arms were covered with insect bites.

By nightfall the boy wanted only to sleep. He stumbled wearily to his place in the camp, and the girl followed slowly. That night the workers received their small wages; they were finished picking in these fields. In the morning the crew would go north to the apple orchards of New York State. The boy spoke softly to the girl as they spread their mats for the night. "Do not fear; I have a plan," he said. "We will pick the apples, and then we will escape." Soon weariness overcame him, and he slept. He did not hear his sister cry herself to sleep.

# ONE

# Sounds
# in the Night

Midnight stillness covered the grounds of Apple Valley Orphanage in New York State. In the darkness of the cellar of Wheelock Cottage for orphan girls, hands reached for two large jars of peaches and then a third.

Upstairs in the girls' dormitory Jeanmarie turned restlessly on her thin mattress. Under it the iron cot springs creaked. Some faint sound had awakened her. She lay on her back once more and listened. The room she shared with four other orphans was still except for the heavy breathing of Winnie. Poor Winnie, always the first to catch cold as the weather turned cooler. The creaking of bed springs from across the room told her that Tess and Maria, the twins, were also restless. She smiled at the sound of one twin, then the other turning. Even in their sleep they were alike!

Maybe they were both dreaming the same things. She listened for Pearl in the cot nearest to the door. Her soft breathing told Jeanmarie she was asleep.

Poor Pearl. Here she was still in the orphanage instead of with her rich, artist aunt. Pearl had gotten over the death of her aunt and resigned herself to not being adopted after all. In the darkness Jeanmarie felt relief overwhelm her sympathy for Pearl. What would she have done without her? Or the others. They'd lost Irene the day after her eighteenth birthday, only that was different. Orphanage rules made you leave then. The two girls who slept upstairs in the attic were seventeen and already had jobs in town. Jeanmarie barely saw them anymore. She closed her eyes. One day she and Pearl, everyone in this dorm, would be eighteen and then . . . the sound of a loud bang banished all thoughts but one—what was that?

She sat up listening. The old wooden cellar door with its tight spring banged loudly when someone didn't hold it, but who could be using it this time of night? She slipped from her cot. Cool air wrapped around her bare legs. Since her twelfth birthday all her clothes felt too short in the arms and legs. Her hair, loosened from its braids for the night, hung about her face, and she pushed the long dark strands behind her ears. Underfoot a floorboard squeaked as she moved lightly into the hall toward the window directly above the cellar door.

Holding aside the wartime blackout curtain that was meant to keep German planes from spotting lights during an air raid, she peered outside. The late October moon shone brightly on the orphanage grounds illuminating the road that ran close to Wheelock Cottage. Across the road, clearly outlined in the moonlight, someone climbed the meadow fence and ran in the direction of the apple orchard below the hill. A boy! At least she thought it was a boy.

Behind Jeanmarie the sleepy voice of Pearl whispered, "Heard you get up. You okay?" Her short brown hair stuck up in little clumps all over her head.

"Quick, you have to see this. Look," Jeanmarie whispered, pointing to the shadowy figure in the meadow running toward the deserted old house beyond the tracks at the edge of the orchard. "The cellar door banged, and I came out to look. He must have been in our cellar. I think he's heading for the migrant workers' place," she said, keeping her voice low. As they watched, the figure disappeared into the darkness. After a moment Jeanmarie let the curtain drop back into place.

Shivering in her old nightgown Pearl hugged her thin arms tight against herself. "I thought all the laborers left over a week ago. Who do you reckon he could be? What could he want in our cellar? Looking for something to take maybe?" In the moonlight Pearl's brown eyes were wide awake.

"We won't know if something is missing until tomorrow." Jeanmarie yawned. "But it can't be one of the Mexican workers. They all move on as soon as the apple picking finishes." She started to yawn again and quickly put her hand over her mouth. "Maybe there's a tramp staying in the place who thought he'd find food in our cellar. Or he could be a runaway," she added. She remembered a notice in the newspaper not long ago about a runaway from Boys' Village.

Pearl sighed. As if she'd heard Jeanmarie's thoughts, she said, "Maybe he's run away from a really awful place like Boys' Village. No one would want to stay in a terrible place like that."

More than once Jeanmarie had heard stories of the harsh life in Boys' Village and places like it. If he really was a runaway she hoped he wouldn't be found. "We can't do anything tonight," she said. A great yawn overtook her. "We'd better get back to bed before Mrs. Ripple wakes up and there's trouble," she whispered. Their former housemother, Mrs. Foster, could be counted on to sleep through anything, but her replacement, Mrs. Ripple, was a light sleeper, and the door to her private rooms was close by. Jeanmarie and Pearl were too far down the hall for any excuse except sleepwalking. Silently they crept back to the dormitory.

Once in the dorm Jeanmarie felt safe. "I've been thinking," she whispered. "Before we say anything to anyone we should find out what's going on. Whoever we saw might be gone by morning, but we can get a pass for off grounds after lunch since it's Saturday. I think we should walk through the orchard for a look around the old house."

"I'm for that," Pearl said. "And for my bed." She shivered as she slid beneath the cold sheets. Jeanmarie yawned again and hurried to her own cot.

The loud, jarring sound of the wake-up bell seemed to come only moments after Jeanmarie fell asleep. She dressed, did her morning assignment to dust and mop the upstairs halls, made her bed, and headed for the dining room. A breathless Pearl met her at the doorway. "Better come and see what's happened," Pearl announced. "Somebody dropped a jar of peaches on the cellar floor and left a mess."

The kitchen girls and several others were in the cellar watching Mrs. Ripple sweep up broken glass when Jeanmarie and Pearl arrived. "Stand back, girls," Mrs. Ripple ordered. "I don't want anyone getting hurt." Though she was a tall woman and broad-shouldered, her face looked smooth and girlish under a crown of silver-blonde hair in braids around her head. As she swept a pile of wet peaches glistening with shards of glass onto her dustpan and deposited it into a wastebasket, she seemed to Jeanmarie like a strong but graceful dancer. "There now, that's the end of it," Mrs. Ripple said, wiping away the last of the sticky juice from the floor. "I imagine the cat must have tipped it over during the night. I'm guessing from the mess, he's cut one of his paws on the glass. Girls, we must make sure this cupboard door is always shut tight."

Mrs. Ripple examined the neat rows of canned peaches, green beans, carrots, Swiss chard, and all the other things the girls had helped Mrs. Foster put up over the summer. Food that must take them through the long winter and spring. "Well, no great harm done," she said. "Everything else on the storage shelves looks okay." She closed the cupboard door and latched it. "Come along to breakfast now," she urged.

When the others left, Jeanmarie and Pearl lingered behind. Quietly Jeanmarie opened the cupboard door. Her sharp eyes had noticed something. "The shelf for the peaches doesn't look right to me," she said softly. "Remember when we had to count the jars for Mrs. Foster the week before she left the orphanage?"

"Right," Pearl said. "She wanted to leave everything just so for the new housemother."

"And since nobody has used any of these all the jars should be here. Only they aren't," Jeanmarie said. "Look." She pointed to a large empty space. "This space is where four jars should be, not one. Somebody's made away with two jars of peaches, and if they hadn't dropped another jar they would have stolen three." She closed the cupboard and stared at Pearl. "Our runaway, or whoever it was we saw last night, must have stolen the peaches."

"Either he is not quite right or mighty hungry," Pearl noted. "After he dropped the jar of peaches, he must have been scared and ran out the cellar door. That's when you heard it bang shut."

Jeanmarie walked over to the door. A shaft of early sunlight glittered off something in the corner near the door. She stooped to pick it up—a piece of glass with a dark brownish stain. Jeanmarie held up the glass carefully for Pearl to see. "It looks like dried blood here to me," she announced. "I think it's our thief who cut himself when he dropped the peaches, not the cat."

"Oh no!" Pearl cried. "I hope he isn't badly hurt."

Jeanmarie wrapped the glass in her handkerchief and placed it in her pocket. "Now all we have to do is find someone with a fresh cut on his hand," she said. Whether he was sick or hungry, she felt sorry for the boy with his problems. She searched carefully for more signs of blood but saw none. "Don't worry," she said. "He didn't bleed enough for a bad wound." Pearl looked relieved.

By early afternoon the line waiting for passes to walk off grounds had thinned to three girls from Ford Cottage when Jeanmarie and Pearl arrived at Dr. Werner's office. Dr. Werner barely glanced at them. "A pass to go for a hike," he said, signing the small card in front of him with a flourish. "Nothing like a good hike to clear the brain," he commented, handing the pass to Jeanmarie. His stern face grew sterner as he looked at her. "Remember that this pass is strictly for a pleasant walk within a reasonable distance. You are not to go trespassing on Gould's Campgrounds or anywhere else."

Jeanmarie felt her face grow warm. "No, sir. Thank you, sir." Dr. Werner had never forgotten Jeanmarie's visit to the deserted camp several months before, a visit that had nearly cost her and some of the other orphans their lives. A shiver went down her back. One more incident like that and she could find herself in another orphanage. Dr. Werner ran his orphanage with an iron hand.

Outside, Pearl whispered, "If he knew what we were planning we'd both be on restrictions, no weekend passes or worse for a month. Maybe we ought to think about this. How are we going to tell Dr. Werner if there are tramps camping out in the orchard place?"

"We aren't going to tell him anything yet," Jeanmarie said. "We'll think of something later if we need to. Right now we need to work our way through the orchard and come as close to the old house as we can without being seen."

The orchard covered a hillside and stretched out farther than one could see on both sides of the road that ran through it. From the top of the orchard hill the road plunged toward a crossroad. Beyond it lay a woods. This time the girls didn't climb the hill but headed for the back of the deserted house. Once they were off the road, fallen leaves crunched loudly under their feet as they walked. The owners of the orchard lived miles away in town, but it was whoever might be hiding out in the old house that worried Jeanmarie.

The apple trees, older in this part of the orchard and thicker, gave the girls some cover, but only a few feet away from the house the trees began to thin out. The house with its two stories might once have been something grand, but no more. Peeled paint, broken railings, cracked windows, and torn roof shingles gave it the look of a condemned building. Jeanmarie swallowed hard. She hadn't thought of it until now, but someone besides the boy could be inside.

She glanced at Pearl's thin, freckled face. A frown wrinkled Pearl's eyebrows, and her closed lips made a thin straight line the way they did when she concentrated hard. Under the freckles her skin was pale. A tiny stab of alarm went through Jeanmarie. "Pearl, maybe we shouldn't go any closer," she whispered.

Pearl looked relieved. "You mean, let's go back and think of something else?" she asked.

In the silence Jeanmarie could almost hear her own heart thumping. "Not that, but we can't walk up to the house and look inside," she said. "Since we've come this far why don't you stay put while I see what I can from that tree." She gestured at a spreading apple tree gnarled with age, whose branches reached out within a foot or two of the house. One of its limbs almost touched the window.

"What are you planning to do?" Pearl whispered.

"If I climb it near to the second-story window maybe I can see inside," Jeanmarie said.

"What if someone sees you? Or you fall?" Pearl pleaded.

"That's why you're here on lookout," Jeanmarie said. "I'll be careful." She crept as quietly as she could to the back of the large tree. Now that she was this close to the house it seemed to her Pearl was right; anyone inside might see her. "Please, Lord, keep us safe," she prayed, leaning against the rough bark of the tree trunk. She put her foot into the first low branch and pulled herself up to crouch in the large Y shape between it and the next one. Grasping the branch above her she climbed higher, straddling the thick limb with both legs. Just as she reached for the next branch she froze. The loud barks of a dog suddenly broke the silence. The barking grew closer and sharper. Someone was shouting. Jeanmarie found herself sliding and slipping against the rough bark toward the ground.

The dog, a large black one, raced at her before she could brace herself for the impact. It skidded to a stop against her and tried at the same time to lick her face. Then it ran directly back to the house and up the rickety steps. Shakily she stood on her feet. The boy running toward her from the orchard was Wilfred! What was he doing here?

A few feet away a stunned Pearl stood looking at them both wide-eyed. "You okay? What are you doing here?" Wilfred demanded, pushing his round, metal-rimmed glasses back on his nose. He brushed a stubborn lock of thick, black hair back from his forehead. "Sorry about the dog. Every time I get a pass off grounds he tags along. I don't know where he lives. You'd think he was an orphan like the rest of us, but he looks pretty well fed. I planned to hike to town before Buster spotted you two. Am I interrupting something?"

Jeanmarie stared at Wilfred. "We should get out of here," she said.

Wilfred's protest "But . . ." was cut off by a shrill scream from the house followed by a loud flood of words, none of them English.

# Two
# New Friends

*T*he screams from the house became shouts as the dog, followed by a boy waving a large stick, came bounding down the rickety steps. The dog ran past Jeanmarie and the others into the woods. The boy stood perfectly still, his black eyes staring, the stick now at his side. Behind him on the top step stood a girl dressed in old jeans and a man's sweater that was much too large for her.

The boy stepped back. "I did not wish to hurt your dog. My sister, she is afraid. She fears the dogs, and this one, he is big and black, and she thinks maybe he is a wild one."

Wilfred took a step forward. "He's not wild, but he doesn't belong to any of us. I'm afraid he likes to follow me around. But how did he get inside the house?"

20

"The door, it was not shut tightly," the boy answered.

Jeanmarie called to the girl, "I hope he didn't bite you!" The girl did not move or answer.

"My sister, she speaks no English," the boy said. Turning to her he spoke rapidly in what Jeanmarie knew must be Spanish. The girl answered softly. "She says to tell you she is not hurt," he translated.

Jeanmarie nodded. She brushed off the dirt and leaves still clinging to her. Had he seen her sliding down the tree? Her face felt warm as she tried to explain. "We live across the road up the hill in the orphanage, and we thought all of you left a week ago. I mean, we haven't seen any of the others working, but I guess you two were with the rest of the pickers." She looked around as if searching for signs of the rest.

From the steps the girl said something in Spanish, and the boy answered. "Señorita, what you say is true. We worked with the others, and they have gone." He stopped and looked searchingly at each of them, his own dark eyes unsearchable. "Like you we are orphans. I think we must trust you," he said slowly. "My sister and I, we have no one to help us. We have escaped, but the danger is not over."

His words startled Jeanmarie. Before she could answer, Wilfred extended his hand to the boy. "Sounds like you're in some kind of trouble," he said. "I'm Wilfred."

Hesitantly the boy took it. "I am Juan. My sister, she is called Serena."

Then Pearl offered her hand, her voice low, "Pearl here."

As if in a dream, Jeanmarie let her own right hand find the boy's. "Jeanmarie," she whispered.

"It is better if we go inside," the boy said.

The three of them followed the boy and his sister into the old house. Once on a winter's night Jeanmarie and some of the other orphans had come this far into the house, but she had only seen it by flashlight then. She could not have imagined anything so decayed and ugly as what she saw now in the light of day. The room they entered might have been a kitchen years ago. It was bare, dirty, and musty, its crumbling wallpaper hanging in large chunks. Black holes and stained cracks were everywhere. The hallway to the upstairs looked no better. Parts of the stair banister had long ago vanished. The place looked as if no one had lived in it for a hundred years, but Jeanmarie knew the migrant laborers who came to pick the apples each fall ate their meals here, slept here. This was their home while they worked. How could people live here? Two gray mice scurried past them darting under a broken floorboard. The boy stamped his foot as if to shoo them away.

Jeanmarie noticed the way he tossed his long black hair from his eyes, eyes almost black. She studied his face, brown from the sun, a strong, good face. He was looking back at her. She felt her face growing warm and turned away to his sister, who had hair like his, thick and black as a crow's feathers. Her eyes too were dark, but Jeanmarie saw them sparkling with tears ready to spill over. She smiled warmly, but the girl's mouth only trembled as she looked away.

Pearl sat down on the cracked, dirty floor and motioned for the girl to sit too. When the others sat the boy called Juan took his place next to his sister. As he crossed his arms his shirt sleeve fell open, showing a white cloth wrapped around his arm just above his wrist. Part of the cloth bore a small blood stain. Jeanmarie glanced at the old wood-burning stove in the corner. A tin pot with no handle sat on top of it. There were no cupboards, nothing else, no sign of food. Once again her eyes met Juan's in time to see a look of defiance, or was it pride?

"Please, you must not stay long. I will tell you our trouble," Juan said. He spoke in Spanish to his sister and listened to her brief comment before he went on. "Our small Mexican village is poor, a mountain village far from the city. A man came to our village to tell us that in the United States my father and I could find work picking the crops. But my padre would not leave my madre and my sister behind. We knew the authorities would not allow our family to cross the border, and so we must find another way. All was arranged. Our family made the long trip to cross the border by night. Six others without legal papers crossed with us. We hid while we waited for Don Carlos, our leader, to come with the rest of the crew, the braceros, the ones the government allows to go." At the mention of the name Don Carlos, Serena uttered a string of Spanish in a sudden outburst. Jeanmarie heard the anger in her tone and wondered.

Juan did not look at his sister as he spoke. "The braceros and the other men rode in an old bus, but Don Carlos made our family ride in his truck. Sometimes we camped in the open, but we did not mind so much. Our family was together, and together we worked hard in the fields. Don Carlos was our crew leader, and we did as he said. He took care of all things. He it was who spoke to the owners of the farms, and for this we must pay him part of our wages. From him we must buy all our food. He made my madre cook for him. Sometimes she would bring back a small piece of meat to add to our beans. Many others had little. Don Carlos threatened to send back anyone who said a word."

Jeanmarie couldn't understand. "But the farmers must have had plenty of food to spare. Couldn't the workers eat some of what they picked?" she asked.

Juan smiled. "The crops belong to the owners. We must work fast, and all must be handled with care so that nothing

23

is damaged. Don Carlos is the eyes and ears for the owners." Juan stopped to brush away a black fly. "The workers must pay money to Don Carlos, and he buys the food for them. Most cannot speak the pure English." Jeanmarie nodded. Don Carlos controlled everything.

Juan pressed his mouth in a tight line for a second, and his voice fell as he said, "And then the fever came." Jeanmarie leaned forward to hear. "First our padre sickened and then our madre. No one could help them. We buried them outside the labor camp. We were camped far from town. When my madre lay near to death she begged Don Carlos to take us back to our grandfather, and he promised he would." Pearl choked on a sob, and Jeanmarie found her own eyes filling with tears.

Juan's face became hard. "All our money was in Don Carlos's hand. He said there was nothing left, but I knew he lied. One night I saw him in his tent counting money from a small leather pouch. It was the pouch my grandfather made for my mother." Juan paused to look at his sister who sat silently weeping. He spoke gently to her and she nodded.

"That night when Don Carlos left I went into his tent to see. There was a letter with my grandfather's name on it. In my village only the priest knows how to read. But I learned from the American artist who lived in my village for one year. The American knew our language well. He taught me to read the Spanish and to speak the English. I read the letter." An angry dark flush covered his face.

"What did the letter say?" Pearl asked in an eager voice.

"Don Carlos is the devil himself. He wrote to my grandfather that all my family were muerte, dead of the fever, and buried here in the United States. My madre, my padre, Serena, Juan, all of us dead." Juan's voice rose. "He did not mean to take us back to our village. For Serena I must do something. We could not let Don Carlos know I saw the letter. We could say nothing. When the time came we would escape. This was our last crop before the return south and after that Mexico. On the day the trucks left we pretended to sleep in the back under the piles of belongings. We hid out in the orchard and watched them leave."

"Couldn't you tell anyone? Go to the police and ask for help?" Jeanmarie asked. She felt a deep anger. Something had to be done for Juan and Serena.

"Our parents made us call Don Carlos 'Uncle' out of respect. After they died he told everyone he was our uncle. We had no proof, no money, nothing. An illegal worker can say nothing. Don Carlos has power because he is the crew leader. The braceros must obey him." Juan's eyes flashed. "Who would believe us? Our so-called uncle would swear that we are ungrateful and a good beating is all we need."

"But what about the police?" Pearl insisted.

The boy slapped his knee angrily. "Two Mexican kids' word against their uncle's, a well-known crew leader? Whatever his story they will believe him."

"But they could call your grandfather," Pearl said.

"There is no telephone in our village," Juan said, "and it is far from the big city. No one will bother." Juan stood up. "Don Carlos arranges everything for the braceros, where they will work, where they will live, what they will earn. He makes all the contacts with the American growers and with the Mexican authorities. He is an important man. The police would only return us to him. No. No police."

"But why did Don Carlos lie to your grandfather in that letter? Why does he want you and Serena? How would he get you back across the border with no papers?" Wilfred asked.

Juan looked at the floor. "He has ways to smuggle us across the border. My sister and I, we are good workers. We would bring in money for whoever owned us." When he raised his head his face was grim. "But we do not want to be owned." He lifted his chin. "We will stay here in the United States. There is a war on, sí? Many men are soldiers now, sí? The crops are over, but we will find other work. In the city I can wash the dishes, sweep the floors. I am strong."

Serena spoke softly, her words melting into one another. Juan nodded. "My sister, she asks you to help us. We have told you our trouble, and she fears."

Jeanmarie looked at Pearl and back to Juan and then at Serena. "Tell her not to be afraid," she said. "We only want to help you."

Juan translated, and Serena uttered "Gracias." Jeanmarie knew it meant thank you.

"In my country," Juan said, "a man's word is his honor. You say you will help us. Then you will not betray us." His eyes searched Jeanmarie's, then Pearl's, then Wilfred's.

Jeanmarie looked at the others, who nodded, and then back to Juan. "You have our word."

Juan's face relaxed into a broad smile. For a few seconds he spoke to Serena, who smiled faintly.

"In my country there are not many orphanages. None so rich like yours. Many children must live in the streets as best they can," Juan said. "Now I will tell to you that I have been to visit your fine house at the top of the hill." Jeanmarie held her breath for a moment as Juan spoke earnestly. "We had no food, no money."

Jeanmarie said. "If it was you who took the jars of peaches, you need to know the housemother didn't even miss them. She thinks the cat knocked one over and broke it."

A dark flush spread over Juan's face. "The cellar door was not locked, and I waited until after midnight. I will pay for them, and the one that broke."

"Then it was your blood on the piece of glass near the cellar door," Pearl added.

"Sí," Juan admitted. "I foolishly dropped one jar. I thought any moment someone would hear and come, but no one came."

Pearl said quietly, "I'm glad you weren't hurt badly. The glass could have caused a nasty cut."

Wilfred had listened quietly. "So here you are," he said, "but what if Don Carlos comes back to look for you? He might figure you escaped from the truck and hid here."

Juan answered quickly. "Sí. But when we came back we did not come straight to the house. We hid in the watchtower in the orchard. From there we watched for the truck. We saw him return to the house. He looked for us and almost came to the tower." Jeanmarie knew the tower. Shaped like a box on high metal stilts and open to the sky, there was just enough low wall to crouch behind. No one went there now that Dr. Werner could no longer spare any of his air-raid warden boys from their day jobs to man the tower.

"We waited until we were sure he would not come back," Juan said. "Soon we will move on." He stood, and the others stood too.

Juan sounded confident, but Jeanmarie's mind whirled. Where could the brother and sister go? They certainly couldn't come to Apple Valley Orphanage. Dr. Werner would go straight to the police. For now they'd have to stay put. "The first thing we need to do is find some food for you," she said.

"There's plenty of apples in the baskets in the cellar," Pearl offered.

"Apples?" Jeanmarie exclaimed. Juan said something in Spanish and Serena smiled. In a minute all of them were laughing.

"Well, okay, you don't want more apples, so what about crackers and jelly?" Pearl offered.

"Right," Jeanmarie agreed. A plan took shape in her mind as she spoke. "We'll fix up a package for you and leave it in the cellar on the floor inside the coal bin under a burlap bag. Nobody comes for coal until morning. You'll have to make sure to get it before then or we could all be in trouble. Only this time remember that the cellar door bangs if you don't hold onto it when you leave."

"I will remember. If you will do this for us, I will come tonight," Juan promised.

Wilfred looked thoughtful. "We won't get another off-ground pass before next Saturday." He pushed his sliding glasses back on his nose. "So we ought to work out a plan of some kind for the rest of the week."

As they talked they walked outside. The dog had come back and stood wagging his tail as if nothing had happened. Pearl picked up a stick to throw. Jeanmarie watched as Pearl bent her arm back in the position of a pitcher. When she let go, the stick went sailing through the air. "Notes," Jeanmarie said. "We can tie a note to a stick, and, Pearl, you can toss it from up on the hill." She turned to Juan. "If you need us you can leave a note under the mat by the cellar door." Juan looked at her for a moment then nodded and went back inside.

The dog seemed to know it was time to go and ran ahead as Wilfred led the way back through the orchard to the road. Back on the road he stopped walking for a moment, a frown on his face. "What if we're helping two illegals enter the United States?" he asked.

Jeanmarie stared at him. "I think they really want to go home to their grandfather, but they just don't know how to get there," she said.

"All we have is Juan's story. They could be runaways," Wilfred insisted.

Pearl had been quiet until now. "We don't really know, but I think it's the saddest story I ever heard."

Jeanmarie tossed her braids behind her. "And I believe him. Besides, we gave our word; remember? In Juan's country a man's word is his honor. This is the U.S., and you can bet our honor is the equal of his anytime!"

"Hold on," Wilfred said. "I didn't say I didn't believe him. It just pays to be careful." Jeanmarie felt her face flush. Wilfred looked at her and sighed. "Okay, okay, so they need our help. At least let's find out everything we can before we get in any deeper."

# THREE

# Surprise in the Cellar

"Pearl, will you keep watch?" Jeanmarie asked as she opened the cellar door.

"Yes, just hurry," Pearl said, closing the door behind her and settling herself on the top step. Ten minutes passed before Pearl signaled in a low voice, "I hear voices coming this way."

"I'm almost finished!" Jeanmarie called back. She patted the last fold of a large burlap bag loosely over the package of food under it. The heavy burlap looked as if it had dropped from its peg on the wall. With a glance at the rest of the almost full coal bin, Jeanmarie dusted off her hands and ran to the stairs.

"False alarm," Pearl said. "They must have gone into the kitchen." She stood up and reached for the doorknob. "I wish we could have sent Juan and Serena something besides jelly and crackers and jars of carrots, don't you? What a mixture."

"At least the food won't be missed. Remember how many bushels of carrots we helped put up this fall?" Jeanmarie said, rubbing a last bit of coal from her fingers. "Anyway, now it's up to Juan to come for it. Nobody will bother with the coal bin before the kitchen girls come for coal in the morning."

Pearl frowned. "But what if Juan doesn't come tonight? What happens if no one comes and the furnace man finds the package? If Mrs. Ripple asks if you know anything about it, what will you say? You know how you are. You would have to tell her."

Pearl was right. Jeanmarie's face would give her away. Mother Anderson used to preach a lot about lying in the Harlem mission where Jeanmarie and her mom had gone to church. "I guess I wouldn't say anything," she said slowly. "But Juan promised. I know he'll come unless something he can't help holds him back. Anyway, I'll come down first thing in the morning before anyone's up to make sure it's gone." She thought of Juan's dark, handsome face and Serena's sad eyes. They were doing the right thing even if it meant taking a risk. She tried not to think of the trouble they'd be in if something did go wrong.

"We ought to tell Winnie and the twins," Pearl said. "They'll want to help."

Jeanmarie stood still thinking. Winnie and the twins would have to know. Out of all the orphans in Apple Valley the five of them had always stood together, sharing the good and bad times. Only now she hesitated. "Juan might be nervous if he thought we'd spread the word about him and Serena to others."

Pearl looked puzzled. "But Winnie and the twins aren't just others. What are you thinking?"

Jeanmarie felt her face grow hot. "Nothing; only Juan might not understand why we told them."

"And you don't want to make him angry, right? What if I was the one who didn't know what's going on?" Pearl asked quietly. "I don't think it's fair to Winnie and the twins."

Jeanmarie stared at Pearl. "Of course we'll tell them. I only meant let's wait a while." In her heart she knew Pearl was right. "I guess I'm not thinking straight; sorry," she said. "Juan will just have to understand. We'll tell them tonight."

They were standing outside the French doors to the game room where most of the fourteen girls in Wheelock Cottage spent their free time before bed. A Frank Sinatra song playing on the radio mingled with sounds of laughter and voices. Through the glass doors Jeanmarie saw the top of Mrs. Ripple's head bowed over a game of checkers with one of the younger children. Mrs. Foster had always stayed in her own quarters after supper until time for lights out. The new housemother didn't seem to mind sitting in the game room with the girls. She looked as if she enjoyed being there. Jeanmarie frowned. Life in Wheelock had changed. The new housemother would be a challenge.

"Look, you go on in," Jeanmarie said, propelling Pearl toward the doors. "I need to write in my journal for a bit. We can tell the others later." Upstairs Jeanmarie pulled the diary from her keepsake box and undid its small lock. It had been a long day. She had just time enough to write in her diary. With the tip of her pencil against her lip she thought about the Mexican boy with his dark eyes. The pencil made a soft sound against the page as she wrote, "Today I met J."

By time for lights out downstairs, Jeanmarie's diary lay safely back in its box. She'd already put on her nightgown—the one with the faded blue flowers and two new patches. Her braids were fixed for the night, and she knew what she would say to Winnie and the twins. Under cover of the noise from across the hall in the younger girls' dorm room, the others listened as she told them about Juan and Serena. Winnie sighed with sympathy when she heard, just as Jeanmarie knew she would.

Maria—Jeanmarie knew it was Maria the twin from the small beauty mark on the left side of her face—said in a low voice, "Losing their parents like that must have been terrible. If they're in danger we have to do something to help them." Tess, the serious twin, nodded. Her short, dark, curly hair and dark eyes were the mirror image of Maria.

"We'll think of a way," Jeanmarie said as Mrs. Ripple called for lights out. It was a long while before Jeanmarie fell asleep.

Waking before anyone was up she crept quietly downstairs. What if Juan hadn't come? She'd slept so soundly she'd heard nothing during the night. Warm air from the furnace reached her as she passed to the coal bin. On the floor the burlap bag lay in a heap. As she picked it up a small object fell from its folds. "Oh!" she exclaimed. On the palm of her hand lay the most exquisite carving of a tiny bird, a perfect little dove. The package of food was gone. *Juan must have left you in its place,* she thought. Could he have made it? Was it his way of saying thank you for the package? She hurried up the stairs, her fingers closed gently over the gift.

A sleepy voice called to Jeanmarie as she passed Pearl's cot. "Everything okay?" Pearl sat up in bed, her eyes wide with question.

"A-OK," Jeanmarie replied.

"It's Sunday; what's everybody doing up so early?" The gravelly voice came from Winnie. Her round face frowned for a moment then went into a broad smile. "Sunday, and the chaplain's away. And that means no choir to worry about. Not that I don't love singing," she added. "It's those horrid hats and blouses that make me look like a two-ton truck I can't stand." She snuggled back under the blanket.

Jeanmarie laughed. "No choir robes, no choir, but don't forget who is speaking. We'll be sitting right out front facing Dr. Werner. He's our minister for the next two Sundays." When the choir sang they sat in stalls placed to the left of the altar and out of the direct sight of the chaplain. The new chaplain, an older gentleman, had a kind, cheerful manner. None of that today, she thought.

"And that means no whispering, no reading, just sitting and staring straight ahead," Pearl said.

Winnie threw off her blanket and sat up. "Do you think the head of every orphanage is so strict, with no sense of humor? When was the last time anyone saw Werner smile? Let me see, last year, I think." Pearl threw her pillow at Winnie, who tossed it to Jeanmarie.

Maria sat up rubbing her eyes. "Wait a minute, what about the package?" she asked.

From the next cot Tess stretched her arms high. "Didn't you hear?" she said. "Everything's A-OK."

"Yes," Jeanmarie said. "And I found something in the cellar this morning where the package had been." She sat cross-legged on her cot holding the small carving on the palm of her hand. "This." In seconds all of them were examining the tiny wooden bird. At the back of its head was a small opening for a chain or ribbon.

"It's beautiful," Winnie declared. "If Juan left it instead of the package he must have meant it as a kind of thank-you."

Maria touched the carving gently. "Your Juan does fine work," she said. "Is he handsome too?"

Jeanmarie placed the bird on the chair near her bed. "In the first place he isn't my Juan. And we don't know if he carved it or someone else. Anyway, there it is. Now what do we do with it?"

Winnie looked thoughtful. "It was you and Pearl who found Juan and his sister and made up the package for them. It really belongs to both of you."

Pearl shrugged her thin shoulders. "Jeanmarie saw him first," she said, looking at her. "Why don't you just keep it in that keepsake box of yours?"

"I suppose I could keep it in there," Jeanmarie replied. "It might be better out of sight for now." She picked it up and reached for her box, slipped the dove inside, and closed the lid.

When the others went back to their beds, Pearl lingered behind. She reached out and touched Jeanmarie's arm. "I meant what I said about the bird. It's yours. I'd sure hate to have to carve that little thing in two." She laughed.

Jeanmarie didn't argue. "Okay, I'll keep it then. And thanks," she added. She wanted it, and Pearl knew.

At breakfast Mrs. Ripple announced that a late hurricane had struck Virginia. Unlike the stern Mrs. Foster's, her voice sounded cheerful even as she said, "So, girls, we can expect this wind and rain to stay around awhile, I'm afraid. Be sure to dress for the weather this morning."

The gusts of strong wind and a cold rain meant Sunday afternoon passes were off. Jeanmarie walked restlessly into the parlor. No one could leave the grounds today. She'd forgotten it was visitors' day too. She watched from the window as the visitors' bus stopped to let off its passengers. There were never many and fewer today. An elderly man struggled up the hill toward James Cottage. The old man turned past Wheelock and went on. He could be somebody's grandfather. Jeanmarie had always thought orphanages were just for kids whose mothers and fathers had died, but it wasn't true. Some of the girls didn't know who their moms or dads were at all. They were orphans in an orphanage, only some were not real orphans. Like most wards of the state whose parents couldn't care for their children and gave them up, she knew who her folks were. She glanced once more at the empty road leading from the bus stop to the girls' hill. Her father had left for parts unknown, and her mother never visited, though she wrote once in a while. Jeanmarie was sure her mom couldn't afford the long bus trip.

She turned from the window just in time to see Lizzie, one of the younger girls, run sobbing in the direction of the cellar stairs. "Lizzie!" Jeanmarie called, hurrying after her. On the top step with the door closed behind her Lizzie sat covering her face with her small hands and crying loudly.

Jeanmarie sat down beside her and gathered the little one in her arms. "Hush now, Lizzie. What can be as bad as all that?" Jeanmarie rocked the child back and forth, gently patting her red curls until the sobs began to lessen. In her heart she already knew the problem. This was visiting day, and Lizzie was so sure that one day her granny would come and see her.

"Is it your granny, dear?" Jeanmarie asked softly.

Lizzie gulped loudly and whispered, "It doesn't work."

"What doesn't work, Lizzie?" Jeanmarie looked down at Lizzie's tear-streaked, freckled face.

The child looked surprised. "You know, what Dr. Werner said in church this morning," she insisted.

"Tell me again, Lizzie; what did he say?" Jeanmarie asked, puzzled.

Lizzie sniffled. "Dr. Werner said that God hears our prayers. And we need to pray to be good. Only I prayed something else, and it didn't work." Tears welled up in her eyes. "I asked him to bring my granny today, please," she said in a small, thin voice.

Jeanmarie hugged the little girl tightly. Then she released her and took both small hands in hers. "Lizzie, God does answer our prayers, you know. But sometimes the people he wants to send us don't want to come, or can't come, and sometimes he has something better in mind for us. He might even be teaching us to be very patient."

"I guess I'm not real patient," Lizzie said. "Maybe Granny couldn't come. She is pretty old," she added. "I'm sure she'd come if she knew how much I want her to visit." The frown on Lizzie's face suddenly broke into a smile with a dimple just to the left of it. She took her hands and put them outside Jeanmarie's and clapped them both together. "I know God's something better part—you!" she exclaimed. "You're my Jeanmarie-Nanny." She laughed and hugged Jeanmarie around the waist. Four of the little girls had nicknamed Jeanmarie their nanny.

"That's my girl," Jeanmarie said, smoothing the little one's tangled curls. She bent and kissed her forehead. "Now run along and find May. She's probably lonely and looking for you to play with her." For several moments Jeanmarie stayed on the step, her head against the wall. She'd forgotten all about praying last night and this morning, and she hadn't even heard Dr. Werner. All she'd been thinking about was Juan and his sister.

# FOUR

# *Danger in the Creek*

On Monday morning it rained in hard lines that struck the windowpane and ran down in streams. A wet leaf blew against the windowsill then fell away. Jeanmarie watched as gusts of wind shook the maples lining the orphanage road to the girls' hill. Fallen leaves covered the ground with a carpet of red-gold, making her think of stories, mostly the kind with enchanted forests in them.

"What are you dreaming of, child?" Mrs. Ripple, though she was a large woman, had moved so quietly that Jeanmarie hadn't heard her enter the room. She jumped and turned to face her. Mrs. Ripple reached out a hand and patted Jeanmarie's shoulder. "I didn't mean to startle you," she said. She smiled. "I used to like rainy days, especially in fall. I'd think of the window as framing a story and make up stories

38

about whatever I could see there. Now, what was it I came in here for?" She turned toward one of the large dressers shared by the girls. "Oh yes," she said. "I mean to mend this dresser scarf this very day." In a moment she had gone off with the torn scarf.

Jeanmarie stared after her. There was something about this new housemother that she felt but couldn't name, something good. Anyway, for now, enough daydreaming. The breakfast bell would ring in twenty minutes, barely time enough for her to do her chores. At least for three whole weeks she didn't need to hurry off before breakfast to the farmhouse. Not that she minded helping Mrs. Koppel, the cook and housekeeper, anymore. Ever since last winter they'd learned to respect each other. Jeanmarie sort of liked the stout little German woman in spite of her temper. But Mrs. K. would be gone for three weeks thanks to her gall bladder operation. She wondered how the staff liked being boarded out for meals in the boys' cottages. Sam, the bus driver, wouldn't mind, but she wondered about the new farmer who liked his food hot and plenty of it. From its hook in the hall closet she lifted the dust mop and began dusting the hall floor.

As Jeanmarie passed by the large bathroom off the hall, Pearl waved the rag she was using to wipe out the sinks. "I've been thinking," she called out, "about you know what. Maybe we ought to ask Mrs. Gillpin's advice."

Jeanmarie marched into the bathroom, shut the door behind her, and leaned against it. "You know we can't do that," she said. "What if she goes to Dr. Werner and tells him everything? Pretty soon the police would be here looking into the whole thing, and then what? We promised Juan we wouldn't betray him. We can't tell Mrs. Gillpin or anyone."

Pearl stood stiffly with her hands on her hips, her mouth turned down in disgust. "Who said anything about betraying anybody? That's not what I meant at all. Mrs. Gillpin's a teacher, isn't she? And a good one. She ought to know something about Mexican migrant workers and the law and that stuff. All we have to do is get her started on the subject, like maybe asking what happens to the migrant workers when they finish the apple crop around here. Questions like that always get her thinking of new projects to do. She loves questions like that."

"I take back everything! You're right. Sorry I jumped at you like that." Jeanmarie moved away from the door and sat on the edge of one of the bathtubs while Pearl ran a brush around the second large tub where a soap ring still lingered. "You are truly a genius," Jeanmarie exclaimed. "We'll find out what the law says about Mexican migrant workers, and Mrs. Gillpin doesn't need to know a thing about Juan and Serena."

"Well, it ought to work," Pearl said, grinning. "And my brilliant mind tells me that if you don't get out of here neither of us is going to get done with chores before breakfast."

The building that housed the school and offices, including Dr. Werner's, sat in the center of the orphanage grounds below the girls' hill. On Mondays classes were always later than usual starting up, and even later today, thanks to the weather. By the time morning exercises were finished and the other students were assigned to their workbooks, things settled down, and Jeanmarie knew this was the moment.

Mrs. Gillpin had come to their side of the room for social studies. Jeanmarie raised her hand. "Mrs. Gillpin, I've been thinking that with the war on, all the farmers around here are pretty short of help. I guess they're glad for the workers like the Mexicans who pick the apples in Blake's Orchard. But I'm curious. Where do the Mexicans go when they finish the apples? I mean, do they all go back to Mexico or do some of them stay in the U.S. and work more?"

Before Mrs. Gillpin could answer, Pearl raised her hand. "I've always wondered how the whole migrant worker thing works," she said. "It really would be an interesting project. Since we have Blake's Orchard right next door practically all of us saw some of the pickers when they were here." Pearl smiled sweetly, glancing as she did so at Jeanmarie.

Mrs. Gillpin looked thoughtful. "Why, I suppose we ought to find out about our migrant workers. It might make an interesting project."

Wilfred raised his hand. "I heard somewhere that a man called a crew leader is the boss over the Mexican laborers under him, and he can be pretty mean sometimes. My question is, what happens if one of the Mexican workers wants to leave the crew and work on his own? Can he do that?"

"I believe there are some serious problems the migrant laborers face," Mrs. Gillpin said. "My, these are wonderful questions, class." Mrs. Gillpin beamed. "Now, I just happen to have a missionary friend in Mexico City who might answer our letters if we write asking about the migrant workers who come here. I fear some do not come in legally. Let's see, we will want articles on the topic, and I'll find out what books are available for us to do some research."

A groan went through the class, but Jeanmarie breathed a sigh of relief. It had worked!

In the notebook hidden on her lap, she wrote "letter" and a big question mark by it. Why didn't Juan write to his grandfather? Why hadn't she thought of it before?

It was still raining after school. This Monday she'd been sent to mend boys' clothes for Miss Toner, housemother in one of the boys' cottages. *Good,* she thought, *I can take the longer way up the hill nearer the orchard house.* She didn't know what she would find, but she wanted to look at the place anyway. Peering through pouring rain she saw little.

Nothing stirred about the old house. Reluctantly she hurried on, sloshing through wet leaves to her work assignment.

On Tuesday the rain continued to fall hard. Inside the class coatroom, Jeanmarie hung up her raincoat. Beside her Pearl kicked off her wet galoshes. "This is the worst rain I've seen. The creek in the meadow is running full to the brim," she said.

Jeanmarie spun around. "The meadow slopes down to the orchard and the house! If the creek overflows it floods the meadow right down to the low places in front of the house." She thought of Juan and his sister. "The place is pretty old," she said. "Do you think the roof leaks?"

"In a dozen places, I bet," Pearl said.

"Rain or not, tomorrow I'm going down there," Jeanmarie announced. "Juan and Serena must be out of food again."

"I could try to toss a note onto the steps telling Juan to come for another package like he did before," Pearl said. "But if you mean to go down there, I'm coming along. When the creek floods it can wash away whole chunks of stuff. It's risky in the dark. We'll need two flashlights."

"Great," Jeanmarie said. Pearl would make going down there a lot easier. "We can plan later."

In the classroom Mrs. Gillpin had placed a pile of material about migrant workers on the worktable. By mid-morning Jeanmarie knew more than she'd ever dreamed about Mexican migrant workers. Wilfred held up his hand. "Listen to this report," he said. "It's about the recent riots in California against Mexicans." He pushed his glasses back and read. "'What began with American sailors using clubs, sticks, and chains to beat unarmed Chicano youths thought to be toughs, spread all over the city and out into the suburbs. One Mexican mother holding a small baby was knocked down, and even the police were beating the youths they arrested. Hundreds of innocent Mexicans were beaten; some were dragged out of streetcars, and many were arrested. The riots lasted for days. Many mothers of Mexican youths had to search afterwards for their children.'" Wilfred paused and wiped his forehead. "And similar incidents happened in other cities in other states too. It looks like Mexican labor is welcome, but some people don't want Mexicans living here."

Jeanmarie felt her stomach turn over. Where could Juan and his sister go on their own and be safe?

Mrs. Gillpin's face looked sad. "Class, these terrible things happen, but not everywhere. The Mexicans are noted for their hard work, their willingness to labor long hours. And here in New York as late as early September 20,000 workers were still urgently needed to harvest the crops. Right now with the war on the farmers couldn't do without the help of the workers the Mexican government sends."

Winnie raised her hand. "But look at these pictures," she said, holding up a book. It was a picture of migrant worker shacks not fit for families to live in. "It isn't fair," Winnie went on. "No one should have to live like that." She turned the pages. "And most of the labor camps set up for them are no better. As long as the farmers get their cheap labor they don't care if children work in the fields all day long." She held up a page from last week's *New York Times*. "Here's an article saying six- and seven-year-olds are working in the fields with the rest of the laborers all day long." Winnie sounded angry, and she wasn't the only one. Jeanmarie swallowed hard. Had Juan and Serena lived in one of those terrible camps without clean water, or plumbing, or electricity?

Mrs. Gillpin put down the book she held. "These are very real problems, class. I'm glad you are learning about them.

My prayer for each of you is that you never become the kind of man or woman who stands by and allows unfair treatment of any persons."

At that moment Jeanmarie could have cheered for Mrs. Gillpin. She smiled as she raised her hand. "I'd like to see laws to change things for farm workers. But I'm wondering, if a Mexican wanted to stay here in the United States and find a good job, would he be able to? I mean if one of the migrant laborers didn't want to go back to Mexico."

Mrs. Gillpin smiled back. "Well, I suppose he could always go home and come back if he paid the head tax, the visa, and medical fees, and of course was not an undesirable criminal or that sort. I imagine many families come together, quite legally."

Jeanmarie's heart sank. Juan and Serena were too young to go home and return even if they could. Don Carlos had no plans to let them out of his grasp if he found them again. But if they stayed in the United States what would happen? The police could arrest them and send them back to Mexico straight into Don Carlos's hands. Even if Juan found work here, life for Mexicans in the United States was not so easy. Where would he go to school?

Pearl slid a note into Jeanmarie's lap. Jeanmarie opened it and read: "We can't let J. and S. down. Let's check out the creek. Meet me at the top of the hill after work. Pearl."

Twice Jeanmarie pricked her finger as she sewed buttons onto newly made shirts while the school sewing teacher looked on. Whenever she found a moment Jeanmarie glanced out the window at the steadily falling rain. In late afternoon she finally finished her work and started home the long way to the top of the hill. Pearl stood waiting. Like Jeanmarie she wore a yellow rain hat tied under the chin. Her long raincoat flapped against her legs.

"Am I seeing things?" Pearl shouted pointing to the meadow. "I think that's Lizzie and May down there by the creek, but it can't be."

Jeanmarie peered through the curtain of rain and saw two small figures close to the edge of the creek. "Oh no!" she cried. "It's them. What are they doing so close to the creek? They shouldn't be here at all. We'd better get down there fast." Both girls climbed the fence and took off running through the water-soaked meadow. "Lizzie, May, come back here!" Jeanmarie called. At the sound of her voice one of the children looked up. Then the unthinkable happened. The small figure who had been standing next to her suddenly slid backwards into the creek. May began screaming for help. Jeanmarie cried out, "Lizzie, oh no, Lizzie! We're coming!" Tears streamed down her face and mingled with the rain as Jeanmarie prayed while she ran.

Pearl outran her. She stopped long enough to pull May away from the water and seat her firmly on a rock. "Stay there and don't move," Pearl commanded. May's screams had become loud sobs, but she did as Pearl said. Pearl ran farther down the creek calling, "Hold on, Lizzie, we're coming!"

Jeanmarie had never seen the creek like this. Its usual bubbling waters were rushing along madly downhill. Little Lizzie had gone shooting down, carried along by the force of the water. "Don't let her drown; please, God!" she prayed. The creek water had washed the dirt out from under the tracks. Lizzie lay wedged close to the rails. In a flash Juan, who had seen it all from the window, came running from the house. He struggled for a moment with Lizzie while he held her face up out of the water.

"Her raincoat, it is snagged!" Juan shouted. Pearl reached Lizzie first. Jeanmarie followed quickly. Pearl yanked the raincoat free, and Juan scooped Lizzie's small body into his arms. Lizzie's face was white, and she hung limp as he carried her up the stairs into the house. Jeanmarie held one of the small cold hands in hers.

Serena spread a shawl on the floor, and Juan gently laid the child down. He turned Lizzie's head to the side just as she spit out a great stream of water. Jeanmarie held Lizzie's head up till she turned to look at her. "Nanny, I don't feel so good," she whispered.

"Oh, Lizzie, you're going to be okay now," Jeanmarie said, cradling the girl in her arms. "I guess I wouldn't feel so good if I'd taken such a swim in the creek either." Lizzie closed her eyes. "We'll take you home right now and get you all dry, Lizzie. Lizzie?" There was no response. Jeanmarie shook her gently. Lizzie opened her eyes but let them shut again. "Sleepy," she whispered.

Juan knelt and ran his hands over Lizzie's head. "There is a bump back here. She must have hit her head. We must carry her home and put her into bed." Lizzie opened her eyes, looked at Juan, and closed them again.

"No," Jeanmarie said. "I can carry her all right. And, Pearl, you can take May home." They'd forgotten poor May all this while. "We left her friend May sitting in the meadow crying her heart out," she explained to Juan. "We better go. Thank you, Juan. You saved Lizzie's life." Juan merely smiled.

Jeanmarie held Lizzie close as they sloshed back through the water. May didn't look up from the rock where she still sat with her head buried on her lap until they called her name. Pearl swooped up the little girl and comforted her as they hurried back to Wheelock.

# FIVE

# Lizzie's Angel

As the doctor was leaving, Jeanmarie, who had been waiting in the hallway, heard him giving instructions to Mrs. Ripple. "Keep her warm. Soup and tea, toast when she's ready. I'd say if all goes well she will be up and around in a day or two. I'll check in tomorrow. Nasty business, this rain. Let me know if anything changes." Jeanmarie stepped aside as they came into the hall.

"I suspect you're one of the young ladies who brought her home," the doctor said and smiled. "Good work. Now I believe you'd better run along and change those wet clothes before you catch yourself a cold." Jeanmarie looked down at her soaked skirt and mud-spattered socks. Her hair hung in limp, wet strands. She had forgotten how she must look.

47

Pearl was drying her short hair with a towel. She'd already bathed and changed her clothes. Jeanmarie couldn't wait to slip into a hot bath. While the water ran she peeled off her wet things. "Lizzie's going to be all right. Oh, Pearl, I thought she was going to die." Jeanmarie buried her head in her hands and let the tears flow.

"It's okay now," Pearl soothed. "Get into the tub and I'll wash your back before I leave." Jeanmarie let herself down into the hot water and sighed. It felt so good. Pearl scrubbed her back and her neck.

"Thanks," Jeanmarie said. "I can't help thinking what might have happened if Juan hadn't acted so quickly." A sudden thought made her gasp. "Juan! What if Lizzie tells everyone about him?"

Pearl stopped pouring water on Jeanmarie's back. "She was out cold when he picked her up. The only place she could have seen him was in the house. Maybe she didn't notice him. Or maybe she won't remember." After Pearl left, Jeanmarie finished her bath quickly. She had to find out what Lizzie knew.

Mrs. Ripple was sitting in a chair next to Lizzie's bed reading to her. She looked up when Jeanmarie entered. "Are you all right, dear?" she asked. "Doctor says Lizzie ought to stay awake for another hour or so, and we're reading stories."

"I'm fine," Jeanmarie replied. "If you like, I can read to Lizzie. I'd really like to."

Mrs. Ripple looked at Lizzie, who smiled. "Nanny, you're just in time to read my favorite story about Pooh and the honey jar," Lizzie said.

"Well, why don't I go downstairs and see where I'm needed," Mrs. Ripple suggested. "I can tell you two will do just fine." She bent to kiss Lizzie's cheek, handed the book to Jeanmarie, and left the room.

"Oh, Lizzie, don't you ever scare me like that again," Jeanmarie said, kneeling by the bedside. She picked up one of Lizzie's small hands and squeezed it. "And whatever you and May were doing down by the creek in all this rain I'll never understand."

"Nanny, we were sure there had to be fish in there. In all this rain some of them might have come to the top. When it rains you know the worms come up too."

"Why, you little goosegirl. I'm certain if there were any fish in the creek they'd have gone under the banks long ago to keep from rushing straight downhill like you did." She kept her voice light as she said, "Tell me, Lizzie, what do you remember about what happened?"

"Well, first I bent over to look, and then I heard calling, and then I was in the water. I thought it was cold and tasted bad, and I was going too fast, but I couldn't stop. Then I think you held my head, and he said I had a bump on my head. I did too."

"He? Who do you mean, Lizzie?"

"You know," Lizzie insisted.

"No, I don't know; who are you talking about?" Jeanmarie asked.

Lizzie was silent for a moment. "Oh," she said. "I guess he must be my angel. I think I remember he touched my head where I bumped it. Anyway, that must be why you didn't see him."

"Why's that, Lizzie?" Jeanmarie probed. If Lizzie thought Juan was an angel she would let her go on thinking so.

"Well, it's because he's an angel that you didn't see him. Don't worry; maybe you'll see yours sometime too. Anyway, I didn't finish telling you. Then you picked me up and brought me home, and Pearl brought May. Then Mrs. Ripple put me to bed and the doctor came. Then I had some tea, and Mrs. Ripple was reading my story, and then you came, Nanny."

"And what happened to your angel?" Jeanmarie barely breathed while she waited for Lizzie's answer.

"He just disappeared. Angels can do that. Now can you read my story?"

Jeanmarie picked up the book and turned to the first page. Relief washed over her. Lizzie had no idea that Juan was a real person. And she must not have seen Serena at all.

For an hour Jeanmarie read until Lizzie finally fell asleep. Mrs. Ripple came into the room with a cup of hot tea on a tray. "This is for you," she whispered to Jeanmarie. "I think it's okay now to let Lizzie sleep." Gratefully Jeanmarie took the tea and thanked Mrs. Ripple. She would need it to stay awake tonight.

Bundled to the neck in a bulky sweater, Pearl looked solemnly at Jeanmarie. "You still planning to go down there tonight in this weather?" The two of them were alone in the dorm, and Jeanmarie was putting warm clothes in a pile under her bed where she could reach them without trouble.

Jeanmarie pushed the pile further under her cot and stood up. "It's the perfect time. Don't you see? Nobody else will be out tonight in this, certainly not Dr. Werner and the air-raid warden boys. With the noise this wind and rain are making Mrs. Ripple won't notice a squeaky floorboard or two. Listen." In the stillness windows rattled, tree branches scratched against the cottage, gusts of wind made their own noise, and the steady rain pounded the roof.

"I guess you're right," Pearl said, "but I know we're crazy to go out there. The pond is probably a lot higher by now. And who knows what else we could run into. Maybe we should wait; but if you're set on tonight, I guess we'll both go." Pearl's eyes pleaded.

"Look, I'll take the road through the orchard and come 'round to the back of the house where the ground is higher," Jeanmarie explained. "I've got my flashlight; I'll be fine by myself."

"But how will you get in?" Pearl asked.

"I'll call and shine my flashlight until Juan comes to the window. If the package is tied to a long stick, he can get it that way. Pearl, you know I'd wait, but did you see them tonight? No sweaters, no coats, nothing but Serena's shawl. They must be freezing, and hungry. Luckily, I still have two old sweaters, the big kind, and I've stuck in a cap and scarves and mittens. This morning I saved two rolls, and this noon I saved cookies from my lunch and Winnie's. The twins added a half sandwich each since they don't like bologna. At least it will help get them through this storm."

Sympathy showed in Pearl's face. "And we can take that man's sweater Mrs. Foster gave me to use as a polishing rag. It has a few holes, but I never did use it for a rag." She ran to the closet and pulled a large black sweater from the corner hook. "Oh, I meant to tell you, I have some cookies too. And crazy as I am, I'm coming with you."

Jeanmarie smiled. "I know it's miserable out there; all the same, I'm glad you're coming. As soon as everyone is asleep we'll go. Midnight should do. You sure you're okay about this?"

Pearl nodded. "I'm sure. We can take turns sleeping till 12:00. I don't mind taking the first watch. If you give me the flashlight I can read under the covers. I'm right in the middle of *Treasure Island.* You can borrow it if you like for your turn."

Twice Jeanmarie exchanged with Pearl. She'd barely fallen asleep when Pearl awakened her and whispered, "It's 12:30—time to get up." Fully dressed and carrying their bundles, the two went silently down the stairs, through the long hall, and into the cellar. Once in the cellar Jeanmarie switched on the bulb hanging overhead near the coat pegs. They worked together putting everything inside a burlap bag borrowed from the coal bin, then tied it with old belts Jeanmarie had found in the upstairs closet.

"There, that should do. We'll have to look for a strong branch when we get to the orchard," Jeanmarie said, keeping her voice low.

Pearl handed her a pair of galoshes. "Better put these on too," she said. "Even in the orchard we'll be sloshing in mud and water." Jeanmarie reached for the galoshes but instead froze at the sound of a nearby sneeze from the storage room.

"It is me—Juan; do not be frightened." Juan stepped into the light, Serena behind him. Holding up his hand he said, "Please, do not be afraid. We came only to get dry and a little warm by the furnace. Before it is light we will go back. I promise."

"But we were just on our way to bring you some food and things. You nearly frightened me out of my wits!" Jeanmarie said in a loud whisper. Beside her, Pearl's face appeared white even in the dull cellar light.

Juan and his sister looked wretched. Their wet hair clung to their heads and both had bare feet. Juan felt Jeanmarie's stare and explained. "We left our sandals in the house. We did not want to lose them in the mud. Besides, our feet will dry quicker."

"Where will you sleep?" Pearl asked.

"In the room where you keep the jars of food behind the large cupboard; under the shelf in the corner there is a small space. On the other side of the wall is the furnace, and it is warm enough there."

"We brought you sweaters," Jeanmarie said, opening the bundle. "They're old but warmer than none."

Serena wrapped one of the scarves around her head and put on the mittens as well as the sweaters. "Gracias," she whispered.

Gratefully Juan accepted the rest of the package contents and the flashlight from Jeanmarie. "We will leave before morning," he promised.

On the way back upstairs Jeanmarie listened to every sound, fearing any minute to hear Mrs. Ripple's voice, but as before only the sounds of the storm reached her. Her eyes felt heavy, but her mind still whirled. Seeing Juan and Serena in the cellar was the last thing she'd expected. What if they didn't wake up in time? What if someone from the kitchen crew or the furnace man saw them? Her heart thumped. She climbed into bed without changing into her nightgown, and with a last effort to keep her eyes open she prayed, "Please God, don't let anyone find Juan and Serena . . ."

The next thing Jeanmarie knew the morning bell was ringing in her ears. She sat up quickly. Juan and Serena—had they left? She had to know. Looking at Pearl's bed as she passed, she noticed Pearl's clothes from the night before strewn across it. Pearl must be washing up. Jeanmarie hurried past the little girls just tumbling out of their dorm. "Oh, Nanny, come see Lizzie," May called, but Jeanmarie hurried past. She had no time now.

The cellar door was open. On the steps below, the kitchen girls were just bringing up a heavy scuttle of coal for the kitchen stove. Jeanmarie stepped aside. "Sorry," she said. "I left something down here last night." She didn't say it was two Mexican migrants.

She waited until the door behind her shut and then hurried to the storage room. Nothing. The space behind the cupboard was empty and without a sign that anyone had been there. She searched behind the furnace and looked into the small cold storage room just to be sure. They were gone as Juan had promised. She felt as if a heavy load had been lifted from her.

For the first time in days, the sun was shining. A robin's-egg blue sky looked as if it could never be anything else. As Jeanmarie got ready for school she hummed lines of a song she'd heard on the radio, "Blue skies smiling at me . . . nothing but blue skies do I see."

On the way to school Jeanmarie buttoned her light jacket. Pearl, walking with her, stopped to turn her collar up. In spite of the sun, the air had a cool nip in it. "Frost coming tonight, I bet," Pearl stated. "Just in time for Halloween. I don't know what I'm going to wear. Have you decided yet what you're going to be?"

Jeanmarie had forgotten all about Halloween and the costume party held in the gym each year. She frowned lightly. "It's only two days away. I don't know what I'll do this year. Maybe we could go as tramps," she suggested. The year before, she and Winnie had won a prize for their costumes as Minnie and Mickey Mouse. They'd worked for weeks on their costumes.

A sudden idea hit her. "We can all go! Serena and Juan too."

"Jeanmarie, you can stop right there. Two Mexican kids would stand out no matter how many kids are at the party. What if Dr. Werner or one of the other staff notices them and asks their names?"

"But if we go as a troop of tramps, we can all black our faces and hands and wear old rags and put on masks to cover our eyes. Everybody does. Nobody will notice two more in the crowd," Jeanmarie insisted. "If we stick together and Juan and Serena stay quiet, I know we can do it. That way they get to see the fun and have doughnuts and cider with us." She didn't mention the apples served along with the doughnuts and cider.

"I know I'm losing my mind to go along on this. If those two didn't need a little fun in their lives I'd put my foot down. We'd better send a note down after work tonight."

"It will be dark way before time for the party. They can slip into the cellar and wait behind the furnace. Once they have their costumes on, all of us can leave by way of the cellar door." Jeanmarie's eyes sparkled as she thought of the excitement of having Juan and Serena in disguise joining in the games like catching apples on a string without using your hands. There weren't prizes for the games, just fun, and they'd all be masked.

Pearl broke into her thoughts. "Jeanmarie, you are a dreamer. I only hope it works. But if I have to toss a message down to them, I'd better get close enough to aim at the top steps or else sail it down in a toy boat."

Jeanmarie laughed. "After work then, we'll meet in the same spot as before."

Everything had gone just as they planned. Pearl's pitching arm landed the small rock with the note secured around it by rubber bands, on the top step. She'd gone close to the bottom of the hill and to anyone watching was merely tossing a stone she'd picked up. Meanwhile, Jeanmarie had pretended to look around the spot where Lizzie had fallen into the creek.

"We'll need rags, lots of big ones," Winnie said later as Jeanmarie explained the plan to the others.

"And brown shoe polish," Maria sang out.

"It's going to work," Jeanmarie said softly to herself.

# SIX

# *Orphans in Disguise*

Jeanmarie bit her lip as she stood silently before Mrs. Ripple. "So, dear, I was hoping you might keep Lizzie close by you tonight at the party. She wants to go, and I'm sure she is quite well. It's just that I'd feel better knowing you are keeping an eye on her. I went ahead and asked if she'd stay by you, and she promised she would." Mrs. Ripple smiled.

"I'd rather not, please." Jeanmarie's words sounded flat and awful to her. But she couldn't baby-sit Lizzie, not tonight. "It's just that I have, some of us have, sort of already made plans. Maybe Leah will watch her. She likes being with the younger girls, really."

Jeanmarie knew she was stumbling over her excuses.

"Oh," Mrs. Ripple said. "I see. Well, never mind. I'll ask Leah. I thought of you first because Lizzie

57

seems so fond of you." Jeanmarie nodded and watched her go. A small stab of guilt went through her for a second. Lizzie wasn't any trouble, but what if she somehow recognized Juan's voice? No! Tonight they mustn't go near Lizzie. Leah would have to do.

Half an hour before time to leave for the gym, Jeanmarie and Pearl slipped into the cellar. Juan and his sister were already there waiting. Serena's eyes were wide as she stared at Jeanmarie and Pearl. Each of them had on long, tattered, multi-colored rag shirts they'd sewn together and dark trousers, actually jeans covered with large dark patches. Their faces wore a thick layer of brown shoe polish as did the backs of their hands and wrists. On their feet they wore galoshes as protection against mud and puddles.

Juan gave a low laugh. "Except for your eyes, I would not know you, señoritas." Silently he held out his hands to Pearl's waiting shoe polish rag. She blacked his face next, then did Serena's. Jeanmarie had brought large patches similar to the ones on her jeans to pin on Juan's trousers and Serena's jeans. Over their old sweaters the two put on the rag shirts Winnie had pieced together for them and stood still for inspection.

"Perfect," Pearl said.

"Yes, and with these eye masks no one will know who you are. We'll all be wearing them." She helped Serena with her mask while Juan put his in place. "Good. Oh," Jeanmarie said, "one more thing. Each of us has a white dot at the bottom of the X on our right knee patches. That way you know who we are, and we know who you are. Not that we think anybody else will be wearing these exact costumes. It's just a safeguard."

Juan looked at his knee patch with its large X and white dot. "That is good," he said. Quickly he translated for Serena. She smiled and nodded her head as she patted her knee.

Just then the cellar door opened. Juan grew rigid, and Serena backed against the wall as three figures dressed exactly like Jeanmarie and Pearl came down the stairs. Each wore a right knee patch with a dotted X.

"Don't be afraid," Jeanmarie urged Juan. "These are our three friends. They know about you and Serena; your secret is safe with them. This is Winnie; she sewed your shirts." Jeanmarie pointed to the center tramp, the one whose costume was definitely fuller than the rest.

"These are the twins, Maria and Tess. Maria is the one with the little brown mole on her face, but you can't even see it now, so I don't know which one she is." Jeanmarie laughed and pointed to Juan and Serena. "And these are our friends, Serena and Juan."

Juan said a few words in Spanish before he spoke in English. "I thank you for all you have done for me and my sister. We will not forget you. You are all very brave."

"It's time to go," Pearl urged. "We don't want to walk into the gym by ourselves. Just remember not to say anything in Spanish, please. We'll stay close together. Just follow us, okay?" Juan relayed everything to Serena, who nodded that she understood.

In a few minutes all of them were walking down the hill toward the gym. Behind them came a steady stream of ghosts, animals, witches, princesses, and strange-looking things like big apples. Ahead of them it was the same. The frosty air held laughter and lighthearted voices. Serena kept her head down at first, but soon she was turning to look at the costumes of those nearby. Jeanmarie had taken Serena's hand to lead her along. By the time they reached the gym, Jeanmarie could feel Serena trembling beside her. She patted her hand and marched through the open door.

The gym was already full of costumed kids of all ages and sizes. A handful of staff people, not in costume, Jeanmarie noted thankfully, moved among the crowd. Apples hung from long strings in one corner of the gym; in another, big tubs filled with water and floating fruit beckoned for the brave to duck for apples. A short distance away stood a ring toss and a bean bag toss, and beyond them other games of skill were set up. Refreshments waited on long tables against the wall. Jeanmarie whispered to Pearl and led the way to the side of the gym with the games. Here they could watch and maybe even play some.

Winnie decided to try her luck with the apples hanging on strings. When her turn came the others watched as, with her hands clasped behind her, she valiantly tried to bite the swinging apple when it passed. Each near miss sent the twins into gales of laughter. At one point Jeanmarie saw Serena laughing so hard she was bent over.

One of the older orphan boys had charge of the game; since none of the staff were close by, Jeanmarie urged Juan to try his luck. "Try," she said. "You can do it."

Juan looked around and, seeing no adults near, took his place in line. When his turn came he eyed the swinging apple and let it pass him twice, then thrust his face out on the next swing and caught it between his teeth.

"Bravo!" Jeanmarie cried, clapping her hands.

Juan unloosed the bitten apple, his now to keep, and smiled at Jeanmarie. As he passed her he whispered, "Your turn."

With her head high Jeanmarie walked to the next waiting apple and nodded when she was ready for the swinging to begin. She didn't see Dr. Werner walking toward the game. On her first try she missed the apple by an inch. On her second and third tries she almost had it, but it slipped away before she could clamp her teeth in it. By the fourth time she was ready and bit deeply into the soft apple flesh. She turned just in time to see Dr. Werner standing near as Juan called out, "Ay caramba!"

Immediately Jeanmarie cried out in the deepest voice she could manage, "Ay caramba!"

As soon as they heard her, Pearl and the others shouted, "Ay caramba!" Winnie, who hadn't quite gotten the hang of it, was a little late as she called "Ay crumba!" Dr. Werner smiled and walked on.

At once Juan realized the danger. "I am sorry," he whispered to Jeanmarie. "I did not mean to call out."

"That was Dr. Werner, the head of the orphanage. He has eyes in the back of his head! But I don't think he suspected anything," Jeanmarie said, keeping her voice low.

Pearl led Serena over to where Jeanmarie and Juan stood with Winnie and the twins. "It's almost time for the grand march," she said. One of the staff turned on the music, and Dr. Werner's booming voice announced the grand march.

"We all walk around in a circle so the judges can see our costumes and pick the winner for best costume," Jeanmarie said. "But don't worry; ours won't win this year." Jeanmarie took Juan's arm and led him to join the line of march now forming. Pearl took Serena, and the twins followed with Winnie walking behind. One of the clowns soon joined Winnie. The music began.

When the music stopped, Dr. Werner announced the winner. He chose two small girls dressed as lambs, all but their faces covered with fleecy white cotton, out of the line of march—Lizzie and May! Jeanmarie clapped with the others as Dr. Werner handed each of them a large blue ribbon. Lizzie beamed and looked around, her eyes searching for someone. Jeanmarie felt an ache. She wanted to run to the two and give them a hug, but she couldn't, not tonight.

Things had gone so well that even standing around with doughnuts and cider proved no problem. With masks on the seven were safe. Jeanmarie glanced at the large wall clock. It was nearly time for the party to end. They needed to be close to the door when Dr. Werner said good night, officially closing the party. Jeanmarie and the others edged nearer to the door until they were beside it. One of the older boys stood by, waiting to open it at Dr. Werner's signal. The instant he did so Jeanmarie hurried out with the others. They had no time to lose. When they reached the top of the hill, Juan and Serena would run past Wheelock, over the road into the orchard, and through the trees to the house. They were running now.

Only no one moved when they reached the top of the hill and looked across the meadow to the house below. Someone was in the house! In an upstairs window a light shone. "Don Carlos," Juan said. Serena grabbed his hand and spoke quickly in Spanish. "He has come back to find us," Juan said.

"We don't know if it's him or not," Jeanmarie said. An idea came to her. "Nobody can recognize you or Serena in that disguise. You look just like the rest of us. We could all go down there and pretend we're trick-or-treating. It's an American custom," she explained. "People always give candy to the ones who come to their door on Halloween."

"Juan and his sister can stay behind the rest of us and keep still," Pearl said. "If whoever is in there comes to the door, they'll know if it's really Don Carlos."

Winnie spoke up. "If it is him, keep still and we'll come back here and decide what to do. At least you and Serena can stay in the cellar for tonight again."

"We will go," Juan said. Maria came to take Serena's arm on one side and Tess on the other. Juan was behind them. Winnie, Pearl, and Jeanmarie went in front. The water in front of the house no longer stood knee deep, but it sloshed around their ankles as they neared the front steps. While the others waited below, Jeanmarie, Pearl, and Winnie climbed the steps and pounded on the door. "Trick or treat!" they yelled. No one answered. Jeanmarie pounded the door again, and all of them yelled, "Trick or treat!"

At the last holler a window on the second floor went up and a man stuck his head out. "What do you want?" he called.

"It's Halloween!" Jeanmarie shouted. "You are supposed to give us candy!"

"Aye, children. I have no candy. I am sorry. But you must go away. Go to your homes." He slammed the window shut.

Jeanmarie, Winnie, and Pearl hurried down the steps. The others were already moving swiftly away from the house through the orchard toward the road. As they hurried, Serena moaned. Jeanmarie knew the man had to be Don Carlos.

Juan confirmed her worst fears. "He has come back to look for us," he said.

"Then you and Serena must hide in the cellar until he goes away again," Jeanmarie insisted. "He won't dare to come to the cottage looking for you. Besides, he doesn't know where you are."

"Doesn't he have to head back to Mexico with the other workers?" Winnie asked.

"Sí," Juan answered. "The others will wait for him in one of the camps. They will go back to Mexico when there is no more work."

"Then all we have to do is keep you safe until Mr. Carlos gets tired of looking and goes on his way," Pearl added.

At the edge of the orchard they stopped. The road in front of them lay clear in the moonlight. On the girls' hill many were still making their way home. Jeanmarie spoke quickly. "We need to cross the road one at a time. As soon as you cross

go straight to the cellar door. Juan, you and Serena hide out
back of the cottage till one of us comes for you. Someone
might be in the cellar, so stay out of sight while you wait."
Juan nodded and translated for Serena. She said nothing.

No one was in the cellar. Jeanmarie slipped outside and
motioned for Juan and Serena to follow her. The two were
soon safely inside the storage room. "Pearl and Winnie have
gone upstairs for cold cream and wet rags to take off the shoe
polish, and Tess is standing guard on the stairs," Jeanmarie
whispered. "In the morning after the kitchen girls take up
their coal for the stove, stay put until you hear the furnace
man come. He brings a helper, and they take care of the furnace morning and evening, always before breakfast and after
supper." Jeanmarie thought for a moment. "In the morning
as soon as you're sure the furnace man has left, you had better come out for the day and hide behind the furnace in that
space between it and the wall. Nobody can see you there,
and it will be warm."

"We are big trouble for you," Juan said.

"That's what friends are for," Maria whispered. Juan
smiled slightly.

"In the morning as soon as I can I'll come down with food
and water. Can you manage till then?" Jeanmarie asked.

"We will manage," Juan replied. He removed his costume
shirt and undid the pinned-on patches from his trousers.
Serena did the same, handing hers to Maria. At that moment
Tess gave a low call, "Company coming" but followed it
quickly with, "It's Winnie and Pearl."

The two had brought cream and worked quickly to get off
as much of the polish as they could from Serena's face, while
Juan scrubbed his own. "That ought to do it for now," Pearl

said, standing back. "We'll take up the rest of the cream for our own faces," she added.

Juan and Serena made their way into the storage room. Jeanmarie had already laid down her own and Pearl's jackets as well as Winnie's and the twins' to give the two something to sleep on. "I guess it's better than the cold floor," she whispered.

"It is fine," Juan said. "We will sleep well."

"Hurry up!" Pearl urged. "It's past the time we should be upstairs."

"Coming," Jeanmarie said. With her hand on the storage door, she whispered one last reminder. "Don't forget to listen for the furnace man's truck to leave before you come out. I'll close the storage room door behind me." Gently but firmly she pulled the door shut and hurried up the stairs.

In the dark Serena let her tears flow. Don Carlos knew they were here. By now he had found the remains of the package the orphans had made for them.

# SEVEN

# Wilfred's Plan

$S$hortly before dawn two figures slipped quietly from the cellar, crossed the road, and disappeared into the orchard in the direction of the old watchtower. Each of them carried a jar of peaches.

Jeanmarie awakened early and dressed quickly. When she crept silently down the cellar stairs and called Juan's name softly there was no answer. With a lump in her throat she hurried into the storage room, then the furnace room, but there was no sign of them. The jackets she had loaned them for the night were hung on pegs near the stairs. She sat on the bottom step to think. Where had they gone? Why hadn't Juan left her a note? "That's it! The note must be under the cellar door mat," she said aloud. She ran to the mat and lifted it. Under it was a bit of white cloth with a crude drawing

66

done with coal. It looked something like a box on stilts. "The watchtower. They've gone to the tower." Maybe Juan felt safer there than in the cellar. At least they could move around, and from there they could see anyone coming through the orchard. With the sketch in her pocket she went upstairs to tell the others.

"We have to find some way to make Carlos leave," Winnie said as Jeanmarie showed them Juan's drawing. "But how?"

"Maybe we should tell Mrs. Ripple that someone who shouldn't be there is staying in the migrant workers' house. That way she could call Dr. Werner, and he could warn Carlos to leave or something," Maria finished lamely.

"Yes, or have the police end up helping Carlos to find his lost 'niece and nephew,'" Pearl said.

Jeanmarie shook her head. "We can't take any chances of bringing in the police. We'll just have to wait till Carlos gets tired of looking. At least he can't stay much longer. His crew is waiting for him, and they'll go back to Mexico like they're supposed to after the picking season is over." As she tried to think what to do she remembered the rolls from breakfast stuffed in her pillowcase. "They'll need food no matter where they are," she said. "We can get afternoon passes to hike off ground, and while some of us keep watch the others can take them a package."

"And don't forget, they'll need a bottle of water too. I can get that," Maria offered.

"Maybe Juan and Serena ought to stay in the tower during the day and at night come back to the cellar until Carlos clears out for good," Pearl suggested. "They can't spend the night out in the cold."

"And they'll need another flashlight since they left mine in the house." Jeanmarie bit her lip as what she had just said came crashing in on her.

"Oh no!" Pearl cried out. "If Carlos found the flashlight and the package from before, then he knows they're here somewhere!"

"All we can do is keep him from finding Juan and Serena until he has to give up and leave," Jeanmarie said. She felt overwhelmed as if an enormous weight were on her shoulders again.

"We'll have to be careful. Maybe only one of us should go to the tower while the others keep close enough to the old house to make Carlos stay inside, if he is in there," Maria said.

"Now, if I were looking for two kids, where would I look?" Tess asked aloud.

"The orchard!" Pearl cried.

"Right. So if all of us are walking around in the orchard it will make his job harder," Tess added.

"Good thinking, but I just remembered," Jeanmarie said. "Wilfred promised to get a pass today and hike over to the house. We were supposed to meet him there. We've got to reach him before he goes. If one of us is first in line for passes she can catch Wilfred when he comes." She felt panic rising inside her. She had no idea how they could keep Don Carlos from finding Juan and Serena. If he decided to check out the tower they wouldn't be able to stop him.

Tess volunteered to go early for a pass. Winnie and Maria went to find whatever supplies they could for the package. Pearl went looking for some kind of wrapping to use.

Left alone, Jeanmarie put her head in her hands. If only there were some easy answer. But what? A small voice made her look up. It was Lizzie. "Are you praying, Nanny dear?" she asked innocently.

"No, Lizzie. But I think maybe that's a good idea." She smiled and held out a hand to the little girl.

Lizzie didn't come. "May is waiting for me downstairs. You pray, and I'll see you later."

Jeanmarie watched her leave. Maybe she did need to pray. Closing her eyes she whispered, "Dear God, we do need help. We don't know what to do, and that man is back. You know all about it, so please watch over Juan and Serena. And I'm sorry I didn't pray sooner. I've got a lot on my mind. And thanks for keeping Lizzie safe." Now, if only she knew what they should do.

Tess and Wilfred were waiting at the road into the orchard when Jeanmarie and the others arrived. Next to Wilfred, Buster the dog stood wagging his tail, his whole black body wriggling with energy. Wilfred looked apologetic as Jeanmarie approached. "Sorry," he said. "I tried to send him back home, but he just keeps following me."

The dog stood on hind legs to sniff at the package in Jeanmarie's hands, forcing her to hold it higher. "Down, Buster, down. That's the boy. At least he sort of obeys," she said, as the dog reluctantly padded back to Wilfred.

"Wilfred has an idea," Tess said. "Why don't you explain it, Wilfred."

"The first thing we want to do is find Don Carlos. That is if he's still around. He hasn't seen me or Buster yet, so if the two of us go over to the old house maybe we can flush him out, or at least see if his truck is still there."

"Like let Buster push open the door again?" Pearl added.

"It's a good plan even if you don't get inside the house. If his truck is there, and he sees you and the dog looking at it, maybe he'll come to a window and tell you to go away or something," Jeanmarie said. "Meanwhile I'll take the package to the tower while the rest of you stay away from the tower but near enough to keep Carlos busy if he's in the orchard. I'll find you as soon as I've seen Juan."

"Tell them to stay up there until we give the all clear," Wilfred said. "Come on, Buster, we're off to give Mr. Carlos some unexpected trouble."

The last storm had done its work well. Fallen branches and wet leaves were everywhere as Wilfred made his way toward the old house. Twice he stooped to pick up a stick and throw it for the dog to fetch. Buster seemed to think it was the main reason for their walk and kept nudging Wilfred's leg to make him throw another. They were only yards away from the house, and Wilfred avoided looking directly at it as he stopped to play with Buster. So far there was no sign of the truck. With the next stick he sent Buster toward the back of the house and ran after him. By the time they had gone completely around the house and several feet into the orchard, he was satisfied. Don Carlos wasn't here; at least his truck wasn't. And how could he be here without his truck?

Wilfred called the dog and led him to the front steps. This time he threw a stick onto the top step. Buster bounded happily after it. On the second throw Wilfred ran up the steps and deliberately banged into the door. No one came. The door was unlocked, and Wilfred opened it.

In a second Buster was inside, racing from kitchen to hall and back again. Wilfred followed him. As soon as he put one foot on the stairway to the upstairs the dog was ahead of him. Buster waited for Wilfred to reach the top landing and then raced down the hall in and out of the rooms.

There was no one around.

Rain had leaked through the roof in several places. Wilfred cringed at the mess of black rot on the walls and windowsills, the broken floorboards, the dirt and neglect all around him. In the last room, in a spot well away from the window, he found an empty bottle, a wrapper from a candy bar, and an empty cigarette package, but no sign of the flashlight or remains of the package or the burlap bag. "Time to get out of here," he said to Buster, who was sniffing at the empty candy wrapper.

In the orchard he met Tess and Maria. The others had scattered to search other parts of the orchard. "No sign of Carlos," Wilfred reported.

"Nothing here either," Tess said, rubbing the back of the hand she'd just scratched on a low branch. "Why don't we fan out through the trees on the upper west side and meet back at the road above the tower?" she suggested.

"Better let me go first so Buster is out of your way. I'll head over there." Wilfred pointed to a section of the orchard where the trees were older and larger.

In less than an hour they were back on the road. The others were just coming in from the north side of the orchard. Jeanmarie waved. "Any news?" she called.

"We know he's been to the house and left. There's no sign anywhere of his truck," Wilfred reported. "If he's on foot he's nowhere on the west side either. And I take it you've covered the north side by the road."

"All the way to the road to Gould's Camp," Pearl said. "Didn't see a single truck or man."

"One thing's for sure," Jeanmarie stated. "Carlos isn't around here, and from the tower Juan can see anyone approaching." She felt some small comfort, but Carlos might be on foot, and the orchard went on for acres on the other side of the road.

"We ought to let Juan know that Don Carlos isn't at the house or anywhere in the orchard on this side of the road," Tess said. "Maybe he's gone for good, back to Mexico."

Jeanmarie nodded. "We'll tell him." The thought of Juan and Serena cooped up in the tower all day long made her angry. She hoped with all her heart Carlos had gone back to Mexico where he belonged.

Glad for the news, Juan and Serena joined the others below while Wilfred stood watch in the tower. Juan stretched his arms. "It feels good to come down from our nest," he said and smiled. Jeanmarie thought, How brave he is and Serena too.

"We don't know if Carlos will try again," she said. "You and Serena will be safe once he goes, but maybe you need to wait one more day to be sure he is gone."

"Sí," Juan agreed. "No one knows which way a snake will go. Don Carlos cannot be trusted. We will stay here until tonight. I will bring Serena when it is safe to come to the cellar. In the morning we will come back to the tower and watch. In two days we will know. I do not think he will come after that." He looked at Jeanmarie for a moment. "We will move on soon, and you will be free of all the trouble we bring."

"No trouble," Jeanmarie said. "We promised to help, and I'm glad we did."

"We cannot repay you," Juan said turning away.

"Friends don't pay. Besides, the little bird you carved for us says thanks whenever I look at it."

Juan smiled. "Then it speaks well."

When they left, the sun was still shining brightly, and Jeanmarie felt sure Don Carlos would not return. Now all we have to do, she thought, is find some way to help Juan and Serena stay in the United States. Someday, maybe in a few years, they'd go back and find their grandfather. She picked up a small stick, threw it ahead of her for Buster, then ran lightly ahead to find another.

# EIGHT

# Spy in the Shadows

On Saturday afternoons a long list of chores for the following week and the names of those assigned to them was posted on the kitchen bulletin board. Standing on her toes to see over the twins' shoulders, Jeanmarie saw her name next to kitchen crew. Pearl's was next to hers. She turned quickly to hug Pearl. "We're on together—kitchen crew."

Pearl's face fell. "I was hoping for dining room duty. All those dishes. How can you be so happy?" She groaned loudly as they backed away for others to look at the list.

Jeanmarie laughed. "Coal, silly, coal in the morning, coal in the evening."

"Oh, right," Pearl's eyebrows raised. "I forgot. Just think, we get to black the stove, bank it for the night, fetch the coal for it every morning,

73

wash dishes and pots, sweep the kitchen floor, and next Saturday morning wipe down every cupboard and all the woodwork. Sounds great to me." Her face said just the opposite.

Jeanmarie didn't care so long as they were the first ones down to the cellar before breakfast each morning and after supper each evening. It would give them a good reason to be down there.

As they left the kitchen Jeanmarie pulled Pearl into the empty parlor and closed the door behind them. "I'm not keen on dishes and pots either," she said. "But I know this—Leah is suspicious. She asked only last night if we were having some kind of party down in the cellar. I laughed and told her I was sorry we weren't, but if we did I'd let her know." Jeanmarie paused to check outside the parlor door. No one was listening, but with Leah one never knew.

Pearl plunked down on the large sofa facing the fireplace. "Do you think she knows anything? Since her buddy, Emma, moved to James Cottage she stays to herself a lot. She's pretty good with the little girls too."

"I know," Jeanmarie said. Leah slept in the small dorm with Lizzie and the other little ones, and she'd seen her helping them with puzzles in the game room. "I've tried to be nice to her, but she acts like she has no time for anybody except the younger children. I still don't trust her, I guess. Anyway, we have to be careful not to let it look like we're going to the cellar too often." She chuckled. "Only now we have a good reason to go."

"Juan and Serena will be coming in tonight after dark, and they'll probably leave for the tower before anyone is up," Pearl observed. "So that means we'll have to leave them a package of food for tomorrow, maybe in the storage room where Juan is sure to find it."

"Yes, but it's just this one more time to find an excuse to go down there, and then tomorrow we start as kitchen crew." Jeanmarie felt like this time things were going in the right direction for them.

In the dining room Winnie and the others were already seated at their table. Each round table sat five girls comfortably. Jeanmarie and Pearl slipped into their places just as Mrs. Ripple stood to lead them in grace. When the last word of the prayer was said, steaming bowls of thick soup were served by the serving girls, who set tables and cleared them. The girls waited quietly until the serving girls left. "Did you notice that Mrs. Ripple doesn't sit by herself at the housemother's table the way Mrs. Foster did?" Maria asked.

Jeanmarie nodded. "I think the little girls like having her sit with them." She glanced at the table on the other side of the dining room where Mrs. Ripple was filling May's bowl.

"Lizzie adores her," Maria noted.

"Well, she is a big improvement over Mrs. Foster," Tess added. "Of course, who wouldn't be?"

Lizzie was talking and smiling away as Jeanmarie watched her. "Oh, well," Jeanmarie said, turning away. "Time will tell. A new broom always sweeps clean." She knew inside that she didn't mean what she had just said. What was the matter with her? She bent her head to hide the flush she felt burning her face.

As Pearl reached for the basket of bread, Winnie's hand shot out to stop her. "Hold on," she said in a low voice. "I was thinking that if each of us buttered a slice and added peanut butter and jam, that would make two and a half sandwiches. That still leaves a slice for everybody." She looked expectantly at each of them.

"A-OK with me," Pearl said. "A half a slice is all I want anyway. Anyone for the other half?"

Jeanmarie smiled and reached for her half. "Good thinking, Winnie." On Saturdays peanut butter, jam, and soup was the standard fare. And apples for dessert, one for each.

As if reading her mind, Tess offered to split an apple, and Maria offered hers. Winnie held out hers, but Pearl pushed it back. "You need it, Winnie. We've all heard you sneezing, and you know the old saying 'an apple a day keeps the doctor away.' I'll split mine with Jeanmarie." When they left the dining room, Winnie's deep skirt pockets bulged with something besides her two hands stuck lightly in each.

Supper was long over and most of the girls drifted into the game room. The radio show starring Smilin' Ed McConnell and his Buster Brown Gang was on tonight as a special feature. Lizzie and May were working on a puzzle with Mrs. Ripple's help. Leah sat nearby watching them.

Jeanmarie kept the package of food wrapped in the sweater under her arm as she slipped past the doorway down the hall toward the cellar. A slight sound behind her made her spin around.

Leah stepped from the doorway of the game room. "Not going to the cellar again, are you?" she asked. "I know you can't be having a party since we're all in here." She laughed nervously.

"No party. I need to check the chores list again. I think I read it wrong. How about a game of checkers later?"

"Can't, I'm busy. Just came out to see if I dropped a puzzle piece. Don't see it." Leah turned quickly and went back to the game room.

Jeanmarie went straight into the kitchen and studied the work chart. Once more she cautiously peeked into the hall. This time it was clear and, without waiting, she slipped quickly through the cellar door and downstairs.

Her heart beat fast. What if Leah followed her after all and caught her leaving the package of food for Juan and Serena? Jeanmarie didn't stop to put a light on in the storage room but felt her way in the dark by following the cupboard until she came to its edge. She kept her hand on its rough wood till she felt the cold stone wall. Above was the shelf with its boxes of summer things and below it the small hiding space. She laid the package down, stumbled her way back to the door into the cellar coatroom, and ran up the stairs. No one was in the hall; she breathed a sigh of relief.

"A-OK," she whispered to Pearl, settling herself into the small space they'd saved for her on the floor near the radio.

The puzzle finished, Mrs. Ripple went to fetch a bowl of popped corn. She patted Jeanmarie's shoulder as she passed. "I'm glad you decided to join us tonight. I've missed you lately." Her calm face was unreadable. But it worried Jeanmarie. Did Mrs. Ripple suspect something too, like Leah?

Sunday dawned bright with sun and high, white clouds. Pearl finished loading the coal scuttle and stood the shovel up against the coal bin. "That ought to do," she said.

Jeanmarie replaced the cellar door mat. "No note, but the package is gone, so I'm sure Juan has it. They probably left early for the tower just to be on the safe side." She took one side of the handle of the heavy scuttle as Pearl took the other side. "Ugh," Jeanmarie said, holding the bucket high enough to miss hitting the stairs.

Breakfast on Sundays seemed to take more plates than usual. The girls who cleared tables had piled the sticky plates high after scraping leftover pancakes and the remains of grapefruit into the garbage. Jeanmarie lifted a pile into the hot soapy water in front of her. The sticky syrup came off easily under her brush. She slipped a plate into the hot rinse water. Pearl pulled it out and dried it with a flour sack towel. Jeanmarie easily kept ahead of Pearl. Her thoughts were far away. This afternoon they'd get passes again and spend time with Juan and Serena. There was so much she wanted to ask Juan.

They were almost the last ones to slip inside the church. Jeanmarie slid into the pew next to Winnie and made room for Pearl. From the pew in front Mrs. Ripple turned to look and frowned slightly. Jeanmarie busied herself with the songbook in her lap.

Dr. Werner cleared his throat. "Before we begin," he said, "I have an announcement to make." Jeanmarie looked up quickly. "I shall be leaving for the city this afternoon and will not return until this evening. There will be no passes for hikes today." He cleared his throat.

Jeanmarie dropped her songbook. At the sound, Dr. Werner looked straight at her, his face stern. Embarrassed, she bent to retrieve it. She picked up the book and fumbled for the page. Her mind whirled. No passes. Juan expected them to come. What would he think? She had to let him know. Jeanmarie had no idea that her book was upside down until Pearl carefully turned it around.

On the way home the five of them walked together. "What can we do?" Jeanmarie said, thinking aloud. She stopped and looked directly at Pearl. "We can't even send a note. There's no way even you can reach the tower."

"You are right. I couldn't throw that far," agreed Pearl. "I doubt Babe Ruth could hit that far."

"Aren't you forgetting something?" Maria questioned. "Juan and Serena will be back tonight to stay in the cellar. He's bright enough to figure out that if nobody comes this afternoon it's because something came up. What we ought to be thinking about is how we're going to help them decide where to go when they leave here. They certainly can't stay all winter in the cellar."

Jeanmarie knew Maria was right. "Maybe not in the cellar," she said, "but what if we found them another place? With some work couldn't they stay in the old house? I know it's awful, but we could clean it up." A dead silence followed.

It didn't stop her. "Look," she said, "it wouldn't be the first time people in trouble hid out in deserted houses. We could bring them a little coal, and there's plenty of wood around in the orchard. I admit food might be a problem, but we can work on that." Jeanmarie looked around at their silent faces. "At least we could try," she begged. "You know some farmer around here will snap Juan up in no time once the season begins."

"I hate to say it," Tess said, "but if they could stay in the old place, how would they keep a fire going without the smoke showing?" The silence continued.

Jeanmarie felt a heavy weight inside her. Winter lay ahead and no one could survive it without heat. "There has to be a way," she said. Her voice sounded flat to her own ears. Pearl shook her head. Tess shrugged her shoulders. For a long while no one said a word as they walked on.

By nightfall a cold snap descended on Apple Valley. In the tower Serena huddled close to Juan. Her lips were blue, and her teeth chattered. They had seen no one all day. Juan spoke rapidly, and the two climbed down the steep stairs. Serena could barely stand. Juan stamped his feet and made her do the same. In the dark they headed for the orphanage. Crouched by the small cellar window Juan peered into the dark interior. As long as it was dark inside they would not run into anyone. Holding the cellar door carefully, he pushed Serena inside, closed the door gently, and dragged her to a warm space behind the furnace. With Serena's head resting on his lap Juan whispered, "Tomorrow we will not go to the tower. We will go back to the house. I will take the metal lid from the ash can and carry hot coals with us. In the small stove they will stay warm for a little while. I will find a way for us, Serena, do not fear."

# NINE

# Lost Locket

Jeanmarie had awakened early, thrown on her clothes, swiftly braided her hair, and hurried to the cellar. Juan was not there. Stifling a yawn, Pearl trudged down the stairs. "Have they gone?" she asked.

Nodding, Jeanmarie replied, "The food is gone too, so they must have left early." Disappointment filled her.

Pearl carried the scuttle to the bin and set it on the floor. "Maybe he left a note; did you check?" she asked.

Jeanmarie had forgotten the cellar mat again. "He did leave one!" she cried, prying the bit of white cloth from underneath. She held the cloth where Pearl could see it. "He's drawn a picture of the old house." Two small stick figures were running toward it. "They've gone back to the house," Jeanmarie said, folding the cloth and putting it inside her skirt pocket.

81

Pearl wiped a smudge from her arm. "That's good. Then we can send them a note today after work explaining why nobody showed up at the tower yesterday."

Opening the cellar door, Jeanmarie looked outside. A cold draft of wind blew through the open door, and she shut it quickly.

Pearl glanced up and frowned. "It's freezing out there. No wonder Juan decided to go back to the house and not to the tower."

With the dustpan Jeanmarie began helping fill the bucket. "They'll have to come here tonight. Without heat they can't stay all night in that run-down place." Inside she felt a growing admiration for Juan. He would survive and do his best to care for Serena.

Dumping a shovel full of coal Pearl said, "Too bad Juan can't build a fire in the old stove in the kitchen."

If worse came to worse he might have to take the risk, Jeanmarie thought. "But with bare trees and nothing to hide the smoke someone might notice," she said, standing the dustpan back in its corner.

They were done. "Ready when you are," Pearl said, gripping her side of the heavy scuttle. As they lifted it, several pieces of coal fell to the floor, and Pearl moved them out of the way with her foot, kicking a stray piece in with the rest.

Jeanmarie pointed to the cellar mat. "Better wipe your feet or you'll track black smudges upstairs to the kitchen, and we'll have to scrub it off."

"I hate this stuff," Pearl said. She wiped her shoes on the mat several times, then held up her foot to examine the sole of her shoe. "Who thought up cream-colored kitchen linoleum anyway? All kitchen floors should be dark enough to hide marks."

"The kitchen is supposed to be bright," Jeanmarie said. "Dark rooms make me think of bad movies with stormy nights and creaky old houses."

"The better to commit a crime," Pearl said. "It's biblical. The dark hides things, the light shows them."

Jeanmarie raised her eyebrows as an idea flashed through her mind. "Why didn't I think of it before? If Juan makes a fire only at night, nobody will see the smoke, right?" It still left the problem of how to keep warm during the day if he and Serena stayed in the old house, but it was a start.

"Now that I think of it, you're right," Pearl agreed. "With heat they could sleep in the old house at least," Pearl said.

"A little coal from the bin now and then won't even be missed," Jeanmarie stated. "Let's leave matches and a small bag of coal along with the food tonight. Juan has all the wood in the orchard he needs to start a fire." She pushed open the cellar door just as someone went hurrying past—Leah! Had she been listening behind the door?

"I smell trouble," Pearl said in a low voice. "Leah's up to her old tricks."

"It looks like it, but we don't know how long she was in the hall. Besides, she knows kitchen crew girls have to fetch coal." All the same a nagging worry began to gnaw inside Jeanmarie as she watched Leah disappear into the parlor.

At breakfast Jeanmarie slipped her boiled egg into the napkin on her lap. When she raised her eyes, Leah was staring at her from across the room. Quickly Jeanmarie looked away. Leah's sharp eyes must have seen her, but she couldn't possibly know about Juan and Serena, not yet anyway. In a low voice she whispered to the others at the table, "I think we're being watched."

In spite of Leah, between them the girls had saved three hard-boiled eggs and two slices of toast with jam. They left the supplies wrapped in napkins and well hidden in the farthest corner of the dorm closet.

The school bell rang loudly. Although it was the same bell that was rung for church, on school days it sounded different to Jeanmarie. She ran down the cellar stairs and grabbed her jacket from its peg. Hers was the last jacket. One of the gloves stuffed in its pocket fell to the floor, and she bent to pick it up. Something shiny lying just under the stairwell caught her eye. A leaf carried in on someone's wet galoshes half covered a small gold locket, the kind lots of the girls liked to wear. Brushing it off, she examined it. On the back were the initials L. S.

Leah's! Was there a picture of Leah's folks in it? With her fingernail Jeanmarie pried it open. Inside was a picture cut from the daily newspaper, a picture of a well-known movie star, Hedy Lamarr. She'd expected something more. Snapping it shut, she thrust the locket into her skirt pocket and left.

As Jeanmarie slipped inside, the classroom seemed noisier than usual, even for a Monday. Someone had spread *The New York Times* on the book table, and a group had formed around it. Mrs. Gillpin stood nearby, smiling. Everyone knew Mrs. Gillpin's husband was a naval officer. The news from the war must be good this morning.

Wilfred, his glasses low on his nose, began reading aloud: "'In a night attack the RAF dropped 2,000 tons of bombs on Dusseldorf, after British-American bombers had unloaded a like amount on other German cities including Cologne. It was the greatest day/night bomb tonnage dropped in aerial history.' And listen to this," Wilfred said. "News from Guadalcanal. 'Green-clad United States Marines swarmed ashore from landing craft early yesterday against fortified Japanese positions in the biggest single Allied landing in this theatre. They quickly had the situation well in hand and within an hour had established themselves between the two main Japanese forces on the island.'" He pushed his glasses up. "'With American naval vessels standing proudly off after a deafening hour-long bombardment, with white columns of water from Japanese bombs spouting in the bay and with American naval Avenger planes strafing the beaches ahead, the landing craft bearing crack United States fighting men wound their way to shore. Japanese planes tried in vain to interrupt the landing.' Whew," Wilfred said. Jeanmarie felt her heart swell with pride as she listened to the war news.

At 5:30, standing in the cold wind on the hill above the meadow, Jeanmarie lost any good feelings she'd had. Where was Pearl? She should have been here half an hour ago. In another ten minutes everyone would be sitting in the dining room, everyone except her and Pearl. The cold air made her eyes water. Wiping them with the back of her hand, she looked once more at the house below. Nothing stirred in the shadows around the house. The note wrapped around a small stone lay in her pocket waiting. Only Pearl could throw it well enough to send it close to the house, and it was getting dark. Reluctantly Jeanmarie turned back toward Wheelock.

About to say grace, Mrs. Ripple frowned and waited for Jeanmarie to be seated. A flush warmed Jeanmarie's face as she slid into her chair and sent a questioning look at Pearl sitting across from her. Pearl shrugged her shoulders in a gesture of helplessness.

"Where were you?" Jeanmarie demanded as soon as she could.

"You won't believe it. Mrs. Tims baked her special cookies, and when I finished the mending she gave me a box of them to deliver to Dr. Werner's office. I planned to hurry back and meet you, but Dr. Werner was just closing up and insisted on giving me a ride home."

"Of all the luck," Winnie said. She quickly added, "but at least he didn't catch you throwing stones." She looked at the faces of the others. "I mean you could say you had good luck, right?" Pearl groaned.

Jeanmarie didn't believe in luck, but if she did she'd call tonight's clean-up bad luck. "Nothing's worse than burned-on scalloped potatoes," she complained, rubbing hard on the stubborn black spots stuck to the corners of a large pan. Mrs. Ripple might be a nice person, but her cooking could stand improvement. The pots had taken twice as long tonight.

"Finally," Jeanmarie said, hanging up her apron. They still had to hide the food for Juan and Serena in the storage room. And someone had to put the coal and matches into a burlap bag. Passing Pearl the coal bucket, Jeanmarie said, "I better go upstairs for the food. We have to make sure nobody follows us downstairs until after the packages are out of sight."

Pearl nodded. "One of us needs to fill up the coal scuttle, and I might as well start on it. If anyone else is down there, I'll whistle Dixie, and you'll know."

Jeanmarie hurried upstairs where the food served from breakfast waited in the closet. Leah looked up from the floor near the closet door where she'd been kneeling. Her face turned red.

"What do you think you're doing?" Jeanmarie demanded. "You have no right to be in here."

Leah stood up, her hands clenched. "Since when is there a rule against looking in here or anywhere else for something you've lost?"

Jeanmarie managed to say, "Lost?"

"Yes, Miss Haughty. It just so happens I lost something important—my locket. I've looked everywhere else. I thought maybe it got picked up accidentally with the laundry and dropped on the floor somewhere." Her voice grew thin. "This was my last place to look."

Jeanmarie knew her face was red. She'd forgotten all about the locket. She pulled it from her pocket. "I found this under the cellar stairs. A leaf had covered it. I meant to give it to you earlier."

Leah reached for the locket, held it in her hand a moment, then slipped it around her neck. "My brother gave it to me when we were kids. I ain't seen him since the day he ran away from the foster house."

A strong feeling of sadness for Leah surged through Jeanmarie. She was ashamed too. "I am so sorry, Leah. Can you ever forgive me? I didn't mean what I said; it's just that I've had a lot on my mind lately."

"That's okay," Leah said. "I don't hold no grudges. Not anymore." She rubbed the locket with her thumb and forefinger. "I'm just glad to get it back. Thanks. You want to see what's in it?"

Jeanmarie nodded. Leah seemed to want to show it to her. She didn't say she'd already opened it.

"This here's Hedy Lamarr, the movie star," Leah said. "I like to think my ma might have looked like her." She snapped the locket shut after a moment. "I better go now." Jeanmarie watched her go. Maybe she ought to try harder to be nice to her. She could ask her to help her do a puzzle sometime. Leah was always watching other people put them together.

She found the package just where they'd left it. With her sweater around the package and two books lying on top of it, she was about to go downstairs when she heard Mrs. Ripple talking to someone in the younger girls' dorm.

"Oh, Lizzie dear," she was saying, "it's not true that Jeanmarie doesn't love you anymore. I don't think she even knows you have this bad old croup."

Lizzie coughed and Jeanmarie heard her say, "Nanny doesn't love me now, but you do, don't you?"

"Of course I love you," Mrs. Ripple said. "Tell me, Lizzie, do you love Jeanmarie?"

"Yes, course I do," Lizzie answered in a hoarse little voice.

"If you love her, and you know what kind of person Jeanmarie is, then you must trust her. Right now something is on Jeanmarie's mind that's keeping her from being her usual self. You must be patient, dear," Mrs. Ripple said.

Jeanmarie stole quietly down the stairs. She didn't know Lizzie was sick. What did Mrs. Ripple mean, she wasn't her usual self? She'd have to be more careful.

When she opened the cellar door she listened for whistling. There was none. Pearl had filled the kitchen coal bucket and put together a small pile on the floor next to it. "I'll get a burlap bag from the storage room," she offered, as Pearl leaned her shovel against the bin.

With the packages safely stowed and the kitchen stove banked for the night, Jeanmarie breathed a sigh of relief. This time she'd left a note with the food explaining why they'd not gotten off-ground passes on Sunday or sent a note yesterday. She also told Juan he could safely build a fire at night. She'd promised to find them blankets too, although she didn't yet know herself where they'd come from.

At the door to the game room she didn't go in with Pearl. "I have something I need to do," she said. "Go ahead and don't wait for me tonight." Running upstairs, Jeanmarie thought of Lizzie. She couldn't tell her about Juan and Serena, but she knew what she could do. If Lizzie wanted her to, she'd read her favorite stories even if it took the rest of the evening.

Mrs. Ripple was just coming from the little girls' dorm. In her hand was Lizzie's favorite Pooh book. "She's sound asleep," Mrs. Ripple said. "Poor little thing. This croup is a nasty sickness." At the look on Jeanmarie's face, she reached out and patted Jeanmarie's shoulder.

"Oh, dear, I didn't mean to sound so serious. We've caught it quite in time, and with proper rest and medicine she'll recover nicely." Mrs. Ripple looked at Jeanmarie with concern in her eyes. "Are you all right?" she asked.

"I'm fine, thanks," Jeanmarie answered. Only she knew she wasn't. She'd almost accused Leah of spying and now she'd let Lizzie down. And what about Juan and Serena? Even here in the United States it wasn't always safe for Mexicans. And some Mexicans betrayed their own people. The thought of Don Carlos and his evil plans made her angry. Juan and Serena deserved better. If it meant sharing food and hiding them all winter she would do it. If only Juan would stay. But would he, or would he leave the way he had come, running in the night? Where could they go and be safe? If only she knew the answers.

# TEN

# *Illness Strikes*

Jeanmarie stared at the full bucket sitting next to the stove in the deserted kitchen. "Someone's filled the coal scuttle."

"Mrs. Ripple?" Pearl suggested.

Jeanmarie couldn't think of anyone else. As if on cue, Mrs. Ripple walked into the kitchen, her hair brushed neatly and a long white apron covering a blue gingham housedress. "Good morning, girls. I see you've already brought up the coal. Good, because I'm planning to make hotcakes this morning, and I need to get started."

Jeanmarie glanced at Pearl, who shrugged her shoulders, as puzzled as she. If Mrs. Ripple hadn't filled the coal bucket, who had? At breakfast they still didn't know.

On the way to school Jeanmarie had a strange feeling as she passed Leah and May, who seemed in no hurry to get to school. Leah had given her a shy smile. It wasn't at all like Leah. She hurried on. She needed to talk to Wilfred before class. Maybe he'd thought of some way to help Juan.

She waited outside the school. Wilfred loved school, though she'd never figured out why, or whether he was brilliant because he liked school, or the other way around. "Over here!" she called, as he plodded into sight, a pile of books under one arm.

"It's you," he said, pushing his glasses back on his nose. "I planned on speaking to you this morning about an idea."

"I knew it," Jeanmarie said. "You've found a way to help them. You are talking about Juan and Serena, right?"

"Yes, and just hold on," Wilfred ordered. "It's not the big solution, only an idea to help out for now. The weather's turned cold, and they need some way to keep warm. I'm thinking there's plenty of old canvas nobody uses stacked in the barn. With rope and canvas, Juan could fix up a lean-to out in the old part of the orchard near the house. The trees are thick and large in there, and it's out of sight from the road or the meadow. With some shelter they can make a pretty good campfire."

"They'll need rope and something to cut wood with, and nails and a hammer too," Jeanmarie said, her mind picturing the lean-to.

"Already thought of those," Wilfred replied. "No one keeps tabs on that kind of thing around the barn. We have old saws and hammers not even used anymore, nails all over the place."

"But how will we get all that to Juan?" Jeanmarie asked.

"Already thought about it," Wilfred said. "Tonight after dark, on my way home from the barn, I'll drop off a burlap bag full of stuff behind the rock on the meadow side of the fence. The big rock near the crest of the hill. You know the one?"

"Wilfred, it's perfect! Now all we have to do is let Juan know."

"When you do, tell him to wait for an hour after dark in case I'm late." He started toward the school steps, then stopped. "Jeanmarie, don't get your hopes up. They can't stay here all winter, not in a lean-to or in that old place."

"And what will they do?" she demanded. "Sleep in barns?"

Wilfred shook his head. "Maybe Juan will find work to take them through the winter. They'd have more chance of work in the city until the next harvest season comes."

"Yes," Jeanmarie said glaring. "And how will they get to the city?"

"I'm only trying to help," Wilfred said in a mild tone.

The noise around them brought Jeanmarie's thoughts back to school. It was time to go inside.

She'd forgotten one thing all this time, maybe they'd all forgotten—Juan and Serena's grandfather. Why didn't Juan write to him to let him know the truth? A letter might take a long time, but when his grandfather learned the truth surely he could do something!

While she and Pearl worked together during project time, she whispered her plan. "I've got to talk to Juan. As soon as we're through here, I'm going to ask Mrs. Gillpin if I can go home. I'll tell her I have a bad headache." Quickly she added, "Well, it is true. What could be a worse headache than Juan and Serena and Don Carlos?" She felt her face grow warm as Pearl looked at her.

"It's a stretch, but I guess it will do. Just don't look at her when you tell her. You're not good at it like some people are," Pearl advised.

Ten minutes later Jeanmarie stood by Mrs. Gillpin's desk, with her head slightly down and her eyes looking at her shoes as she made her request. Mrs. Gillpin placed a cool hand on Jeanmarie's forehead. "You don't feel feverish, my dear. But I know a bad headache doesn't need a fever to make one sick. Do you want someone to walk you home?"

"No thanks," Jeanmarie said in her lowest voice.

"Well then, you go ahead, and you can tell Mrs. Ripple I sent you home. I'll telephone later at lunchtime."

Jeanmarie made herself walk slowly to the coatroom. She liked Mrs. Gillpin, and she really couldn't have looked her in the eye and said what she did. The cold air that nipped at her face as she opened the door felt good. She still had a half hour before Mrs. Gillpin telephoned. Enough time to talk to Juan.

Out of breath with hurrying and worrying for fear someone would see her, Jeanmarie crossed the road long before coming in sight of Wheelock. Running between the trees she came quickly to the house. No one came when she knocked. The door opened easily. Calling, she ran from room to room, then upstairs too. They were gone! Maybe Juan had decided to go to the tower and watch from there. She had to know.

The tower was empty. Jeanmarie felt suddenly empty too, and cold. They were really gone! She trudged toward Wheelock, no longer caring who saw her. Mechanically she opened the cellar door and went to hang up her jacket. The door to the storage room was shut, the cellar empty. Then someone sneezed.

Jeanmarie froze. Silence followed, but a sudden instinct made her go into the furnace room. "Psst, Juan, is that you?" she whispered.

From behind the furnace came sounds of scrambling, and Juan appeared. He looked rumpled and weary. "Sí, we are here," he whispered.

Jeanmarie's stomach felt like it had turned a cartwheel. "I looked everywhere for you," she said. "What are you doing here?"

"Serena is sick with the fever. I could not keep her in the house in the cold. Tonight I will build a fire, and when it is warm enough, I will bring her there. I am sorry to cause you trouble."

"Oh no, I'm glad you are here," Jeanmarie said. "I'm supposed to be home with a headache so I can't stay long. Here, take my jacket and scarf for her. You'd both better move into the storage room. It's safer there once school is out." A low moan came from behind the furnace.

"Wait; I will get Serena," Juan said.

The girl looked weak and ill as Juan helped her to the storage room. Jeanmarie laid down burlap bags behind the large cupboard. Wrapped in Jeanmarie's jacket and scarf, Serena lay on the homemade bed. Jeanmarie smoothed the girl's dark hair from her forehead. "She's hot with fever," she whispered. "I'll get medicine for her and come back as soon as I can. You're safe in here," she reassured Juan. "Last night Mrs. Ripple brought up all the supplies she needed for tonight's stew."

"Gracias," Juan whispered. "We can never repay you for your help. Gracias." Heavy circles ringed his eyes, and his face had an ashen look to Jeanmarie.

"Get some sleep yourself," she said. "When I come I'll rap the door with two short knocks, then wait and repeat them so you'll know it's me." Juan nodded wearily.

Mrs. Ripple emerged from her sewing room as Jeanmarie came upstairs to the dorm. "Jeanmarie, is that you? Mrs. Gillpin called not long ago to tell me she sent you home." Mrs. Ripple looked sympathetic. She touched Jeanmarie's face. "You're not warm, thankfully. Maybe a good nap will help, dear. Did you sleep well last night? Does your stomach feel sick too?"

Jeanmarie answered no to the last question and added, "Do you think I can have some aspirin, please? It always seems to help."

"Of course, dear. Wait here while I fetch them." In moments Mrs. Ripple returned with two aspirin tablets and a glass of water. "Why don't you take these and then lie down for a little nap. I'll be right here in my sewing room. Just call me if you need me."

Jeanmarie took the glass and the aspirin. "Thank you. I'll keep the glass by my bed," she said. Before Mrs. Ripple could say anything, Jeanmarie turned and went straight into the dorm. Quickly she slipped the pills into her skirt pocket and drank the glass of water. Slipping off her shoes she lay on her cot and closed her eyes. For now she had no other choice.

At 3:00 Mrs. Ripple brought her tea and a slice of toast. "Feeling any better?" she asked, setting the tea on the nightstand next to Jeanmarie's bed.

"Yes, I think I am." Jeanmarie sat up. She had actually fallen asleep.

"Well, try eating something and if you still feel well, perhaps your headache is really over." Mrs. Ripple left and Jeanmarie sipped the hot tea. Thoughts of Serena pressed her. It was Serena who needed the hot tea and the aspirin, but Mrs. Ripple would be in the kitchen. She would have to wait.

Close to suppertime Jeanmarie brushed her hair, straightened her skirt, and took the tea things back to the kitchen.

Mrs. Ripple smiled, her face rosy with heat from the oven as she lifted a pan of hot rolls. "I'm glad to see you looking rested," she said. "Can you join us for supper?"

"Yes, I think so. The food smells good, and my headache's gone. Thanks for the tea," Jeanmarie said. In the dining room steaming bowls of chicken noodle soup, fragrant with green herbs, waited next to heaps of hot rolls. Cottage cheese, canned peaches, milk, and peanut butter cookies completed the meal. Jeanmarie was hungry. She tried not to hurry, but all she could think of was Serena. When Mrs. Ripple rose, signaling that supper was over, Jeanmarie waited till most of the girls left.

The girls clearing tables were already at work. As soon as they finished, Jeanmarie hurried to the kitchen. As she began putting leftover soup into a bowl, her hand trembled, spilling some onto the floor. She stared at the spill, her thoughts on Serena. "Oh, Pearl, what if Serena is really sick and needs a doctor? What can we do?"

Pearl bent to wipe up the spill. "I don't know," she said. "The sooner you get some of this broth to her the better. You go ahead, and I'll cover for you." She laid a clean plate over the top of the bowl of soup and placed it in the empty coal scuttle, added spoons, two hot rolls, a small jar of milk, and a jar of water, and laid a sheet of newspaper over it all. "Now go," Pearl urged. "I'll keep an eye out from the kitchen. If anyone comes I'll make sure I come down first."

Jeanmarie could feel her throat tightening up. The hallway was empty, and she quickly slipped down the cellar stairs, closing the door behind her. After her second rap on the storage door it opened. Jeanmarie went in, shutting it behind her. When she pulled the light on, Juan blinked in the sudden brightness.

Jeanmarie set the food down. "I came as soon as I could." She held out the tablets and the jar of water. "It's aspirin; maybe it will help."

Serena opened her eyes, squinting at the light. Juan knelt and helped her sit up as Jeanmarie coaxed her to take the aspirin and held the water to her lips. "Gracias," Serena whispered. She said something more in Spanish.

Juan translated. "She says it was the cold that chilled her and brought on the fever. If we can stay here for tonight she is sure she will be better tomorrow." He added a few words in Spanish and Serena nodded.

While Juan ate his soup, Jeanmarie fed spoonfuls of the broth to Serena who took a little before signaling she wanted no more.

"Juan, I need to talk to you," Jeanmarie said. She explained about Wilfred's idea.

"It is a good idea," Juan said. "But I think we must go soon to the city and find work. We cannot stay here in the winter. I will go to the house tonight, but Serena must stay here." He explained briefly to Serena.

Her eyes grew wide as she grasped Juan's arm and spoke in a pleading voice.

"She does not want to stay here alone," Juan said.

"Tell her I'll stay with her tonight," Jeanmarie said. "As soon as it's safe I'll come, and you can leave then."

Juan looked at her in surprise. "You will do this for us?"

"I'm glad to," Jeanmarie said and smiled at Serena.

Juan translated while Serena stared at Jeanmarie. When he was finished she nodded and closed her eyes. As Juan watched his sister, Jeanmarie saw a look of tenderness cross his face. "Tonight," Juan said, "I will build a fire in the stove to warm the kitchen. I will come for Serena before dawn." Jeanmarie nodded. Juan held the door for her as she left and closed it behind her.

With a towel around the empty dishes she carried them upstairs. From the kitchen Pearl saw her coming and hurried to take them from her. Maria was drying dishes, Tess putting them away, and Winnie already sweeping the floor.

In a low voice Jeanmarie filled them in on Serena and Juan. All of them agreed with Jeanmarie's plan and offered to keep watch with her until midnight.

"Time to go," Tess whispered. She had drawn the last watch and gently shook Jeanmarie awake. Fully dressed, Jeanmarie threw back the bedspread. Tess proceeded to stuff pillows under it into mounds to look like someone asleep under the covers. Jeanmarie signaled her thanks and left quietly.

# ELEVEN

# Night Vigil

With two blankets and Pearl's old flashlight under one arm, Jeanmarie crept down the stairs, letting the railing guide her in the dark. Tonight no storm or high winds muffled the squeaking step under her foot, and she waited motionless, listening. Nothing moved in the stillness around her. At the cellar door she lifted the knob, pressing it up to keep the door from making noise, then closed it gently behind her.

Juan was waiting by the storage room door.

Jeanmarie held out one of the blankets and the flashlight. "Take these. You'll need them."

Juan shook his head. "No, you will need the light and the blankets for you and Serena." In a moment he was gone. Behind him cold night air swept into the room from the opening of the door. Jeanmarie wished Juan had taken the blanket. The thought that he would make a fire brought her some comfort.

99

In the storage room the light was on. Serena sat leaning against the wall. Jeanmarie laid the blankets on her lap, touching the girl's hand lightly. Serena ran her fingers over the rough wool and nodded her thanks. Jeanmarie switched on her flashlight and turned off the overhead light.

"Por favor, por favor," Serena whispered, holding out one of the blankets. She had wrapped the other one around herself. Jeanmarie took the blanket, draped it around like a long shawl, and crawled in next to Serena. Under them the burlap bags covered the cement floor. Jeanmarie laid the flashlight by her side and switched it off. Thick darkness enveloped them. Nothing was visible. No wonder Serena hadn't wanted to stay alone. In the cramped space she could feel Serena close to her. She could hear her breathing and something else. Serena was crying.

In the darkness Jeanmarie reached out to comfort her. She felt the warm tears on Serena's face and wiped them with her hand. "Don't be afraid," she whispered. She knew one line of Spanish from a song she'd heard; she whispered it softly, "Vaya con Dios." Serena clung to her, and Jeanmarie cradled the younger girl in her arms. When Juan woke them, Jeanmarie's arm felt numb from holding Serena, and her back and legs were stiff.

"While it is still dark, we must go," he said. Serena rose and began to unwrap the blanket. Jeanmarie stopped her gently. "No, no. You must take it. These are both for you," she said, handing the other one to Juan. "And you must take food with you." She hurried back into the storage room. "Put these on top of the bag of coal," she said, giving Juan a jar of peaches and another of corn. "This one is syrup we use to sweeten food, but it's good for coughs." Jeanmarie placed the last jar in Serena's hands.

Juan had draped the second blanket over Serena's head and shoulders. "Vaya con Dios," she whispered as they left. Jeanmarie nodded. When the door closed behind them she crept quietly upstairs, her legs heavy and her eyes watering. She could hardly wait to fall into her own lumpy bed.

In the morning Jeanmarie awakened to Winnie's hand shaking her shoulder. "Wake up. We're dying to know how it went last night."

Jeanmarie groaned as she sat up. "They've gone to the house, if that's what you want to know," she said. Her body wanted at least another hour of sleep even though she'd slept right through the wake-up bell.

"What about Serena?" Pearl insisted.

Jeanmarie found herself suddenly awake as she looked at Pearl. "The medicine and hot broth helped some, but she needs more."

Pearl put her hands on her hips. "You aren't planning to stay home from school again today?" she asked.

Jeanmarie stood up gingerly. She felt just like staying home. "I can't. If I don't go to school I'll be here with Mrs. Ripple. No. Somebody has to leave school and go by the old house on their way home. If we can get the aspirin before school it should work." Jeanmarie looked at Pearl.

"Oh no, not me." Pearl backed away. "I never get headaches, and besides, two headaches in two days will make even Mrs. Gillpin suspicious."

"Not a headache this time," Jeanmarie said. "You do get stomach upsets once in a while. Think of Serena, Pearl. You can do it this one time," she urged.

"Even if I could, what good would it do? No one gives out aspirins for an upset stomach," Pearl said.

"Well then, what about a cold?" Jeanmarie said quickly. Pearl didn't have one, but she knew who did. She looked at Winnie. "Don't you have a cold, Winnie?"

"Well, yes, but what good will that do us?" Winnie's eyebrows rose quizzically.

"Colds, light sinus headache?" Jeanmarie questioned. "All you need to do is tell Mrs. Ripple your colds sometimes end in sinus problems; they do, you know, Win. And two aspirins before school would help. They'll help Serena."

Winnie's face looked pained. "I thought you were sleeping late this morning, but you were just laying there planning how we could all end up in trouble." She paused a moment. "I suppose it won't hurt this once, and I wouldn't do it if that poor girl didn't need help."

At mid-morning, with the medicine wrapped in a hanky and parts of five lunches bulging out the pockets of her coat, Pearl left school. She'd done her part just as they'd planned. In her hand was the note from Mrs. Gillpin, dismissing her for the day. Now if all went well she'd make a quick delivery to Juan and Serena at the old house and be on her way home. After that she'd spend the rest of the day reading in bed. It mightn't be so bad after all.

Near the road to the orchard she sprinted lightly through the small woods near Wheelock, across, and into the orchard. In the gray, overcast day she barely noticed the wisps of smoke coming from the chimney of the old house.

Juan opened the door to her knock, and she went inside. The kitchen stove sent out warmth, and Serena huddled close to it. With few words Pearl thrust the food and medicine into Juan's hands. "You will stay here tonight?" she asked.

"Sí," Juan answered. "I have plenty of wood. We will stay here."

"All right then, Jeanmarie will bring you food tonight after dark. I have to go now." Relief washed over Pearl as she ran once more through the orchard toward home.

Though the day had gone as they'd planned, Jeanmarie felt a gnawing fear inside her. Don Carlos was gone, and Serena would get well, but it meant Juan might decide to leave soon. In the cellar she slipped her jacket on and picked up the jar of water and the bundle of food. Upstairs Pearl was making popcorn for everyone, and Winnie and the twins had challenged Mrs. Ripple to a long game of Monopoly. Jeanmarie closed the cellar door quietly behind her.

She decided to go by way of the meadow this time rather than through the orchard in the dark. At this time of night no one was about on the orphanage grounds. The heavy blackout curtains hid the lights she knew were on inside the cottages. Thick cardboard over the windows shut out any light from inside the old house as she approached. If only she could persuade Juan to stay.

Inside the kitchen a warm fire glowed in the small stove. Seated on a small log, and Serena on another close to the stove, Jeanmarie listened to Juan. He had written his grandfather many weeks ago, telling him the truth of his and Serena's plight and Don Carlos's treachery.

"I had no address to give him," Juan said, pacing back and forth as he spoke. "I knew only that we traveled always north, following the crops to the last one, the apples in New York. I promised him we would return one day."

Jeanmarie felt Juan's sadness when he spoke of his grandfather. At least he knew his grandchildren were alive. But what could the poor old man do so far away and with no idea where to find them?

When she left a few minutes later, her thoughts were full of Juan's words. She retraced her steps toward Wheelock, unaware that anyone saw.

In the orchard slightly off the road a truck sat with its lights off. Inside, a man watched Jeanmarie struggle across the meadow.

# TWELVE

# *Terror in the Dark*

The hours passed, and still the man in the truck waited. At last he lit a match and held it close to his pocket watch. It was past midnight. He left the truck, carefully closing the door to make no sound. Nothing stirred near the old house. Without a lock the door opened easily and silently. The fire, banked for the night, sent out flickers of light through the small stove door. On the floor two figures lay sleeping. The man stood above the smaller one and gave a sharp nudge with his boot.

Serena opened her eyes, stared at the face above her, and screamed. Instantly Juan came awake, but already a heavy boot against his chest pinned him to the floor. Don Carlos!

"Children, children," he said with his foot still on Juan. "How could you be so ungrateful to your poor uncle? I went on without you, but my heart smote me to think of your dear madre's last words." He pressed harder against Juan, causing pain, and Juan lay still. "Did I not promise her I would care for you?" Juan said nothing. Serena sobbed quietly.

Don Carlos drew out a wicked-looking knife, at the same time releasing Juan. Waving the knife in his hand Don Carlos motioned for Juan to sit up. With a glance in Serena's direction Juan obeyed.

"From now on you will do as I say or you will find yourself very sorry." He leaned forward and tapped Juan's shoulder with his knife. "I am your uncle, and you are in my care. You understand, no?" Juan nodded. "That goes for both of you," Don Carlos said. "Come, come, little one, dry your tears. You must make your madre proud of you. She would want you to learn much, work hard. And one day you will marry a fine worker and raise many children." Serena could not look at him and kept her head bowed.

Don Carlos turned to Juan. "I could have left you, you fool. Do you think you could stay here in this place forever? Or were you planning to run away to the city? Did you not hear how the gringos rounded up every Mexican boy and girl they saw last year in the big city of Los Angeles? They arrested them, beat them for nothing. Women and children too. We are good for the fields, but they do not want us to live with them. Is that what you want, eh?" His voice grew softer, wheedling as he squatted before Juan. "Think, boy, of your sister. Think of her."

Juan could hold back no longer. "You speak of the gringos, but you lied to my grandfather. Are we dead, my sister and I? I saw the letter." Juan's whole body trembled. "You did not know I read the Spanish and speak the English."

Surprise filled Don Carlos's face as he stood up. "So you know?" After a moment he sat down on a log. "Maybe I did wrong," he said. "I lied to your grandfather, but I thought it was the best way. Quick, a clean break. He will accept it. Would you have him die worrying about you and your sister?" He placed the knife back in his belt. "I cannot take you back to your village." The words fell flat to Juan's ears. "Once we cross into Mexico I have things I must do. After that I will begin again to make ready for the new season. In some places the braceros stay here all year, and it is legal. But the farmers, they ask me to bring them cheap labor and promise me they will hire as many as I can bring, legal and illegal. The mix is good for them and for me. I have my papers, and the authorities know me. I come and go without questions. A little money here and there—no questions asked." He stopped and stared at Juan. "No one will take you to your village. On your own you know what will happen to you before you reach home. Who will you trust? The child-stealers? The authorities? Do they bother with peons or children?"

He leaned close to Juan. "Have sense, boy. Your best lot is with me. I will teach you many things. Your sister will be unharmed."

Juan felt his mind reeling. In his heart he knew that much of what Don Carlos said was true. He tried to think. Did Carlos mean to help them or something worse? No matter what he said, the lie to his grandfather was wrong. He would never forgive him.

Carlos fished a candy bar from his pocket and broke it in half. He placed half near Juan and the other half in Serena's lap. "Eat, little one. Tomorrow we will go back to Mexico and the good tortillas. The drive will be long." He reached a hand to pat Serena's head. She did not look up. "Never mind, little one. I know you grieve for your madre and padre. It is a sad world. I will do my best to look after you." His words, spoken in Spanish, brought fresh tears to Serena, but this time she lay down and pulled the blanket close around her. In her hand she held the uneaten candy.

Don Carlos smiled and patted her shoulder. "One thing I must have from you, boy," he said. "You must give me your word of honor that you will not try to run away again. I promise you I will take care of you both, and I will teach you myself the things you must know in these times." He extended his hand to Juan.

Juan had no more fight left. He took Don Carlos's hand. "I promise," he said. It was done. For Serena's sake he would keep his promise.

Don Carlos gripped his shoulder. "You are a man of honor. Sleep now and in the morning we will take our leave." In the dark lying by the stove, Carlos said wearily, "We are in good luck, boy. We have a full load of American cigarettes, nylons, things that will sell well in Mexico City. I will teach you the trade."

"But how will you get these things across the border?" Juan asked. He had to know.

"Already you are asking the good questions." Don Carlos sounded pleased. "In the bottom of the back of the truck is a secret compartment." He laughed. "You see, even you did not know and you rode there."

Juan lay still, his eyes open. Don Carlos was a smuggler, a liar, and a thief. How could he have forgotten his madre's money? He saw Don Carlos steal it with his own eyes. Maybe the man had two sides to him. He had come back for them, and he had promised to take care of them. But in his heart Juan knew he could not trust Don Carlos.

He rolled over on his side and sat up partway. "Don Carlos, I must go outside of necessity. I have given you my word of honor."

Carlos sat up. "I have no doubt you will return. There is nowhere else to go. Serena and I will be here waiting."

Carlos knew Juan would not leave Serena. "I will take the flashlight the orphans left for us," Juan said.

"Go," Carlos said impatiently. "And in the morning we will return the flashlight and the blankets to the gringos. We will leave them no reason to follow us."

Outside Juan went swiftly to the back of the house. Quickly he tore a small piece from the cloth around his arm. The cut was healed but Juan kept it covered. He laid the flashlight on the ground and spread the cloth next to it. From his pocket he took the piece of charcoal he had used for his other notes and in the dull light sketched a truck. A dark arrow pointed to the back of the truck. Quickly he sketched a flatbed under the truck and small packets marked with X's. He added two stick figures, put large X's where mouths would be, and drew hands tied together in front of the figures. Folding the cloth he unscrewed the top of the flashlight and placed it over the bulb and screwed back the top. Now if only Carlos did not try to use the flashlight tonight, the note might reach Jean-marie safely. In the morning he would fold the blankets, roll them with the flashlight inside, and tie the roll with a strip of string. He could only pray she would find it and understand.

Back inside the house Carlos greeted him in a low voice. "You must try to sleep," he said. "Once you learn to drive the truck, we will not need to make long stops."

Did Carlos think to bribe him by promising to teach him to drive? Juan turned over on his side and closed his eyes. He trusted nothing Carlos said, but he would go along for Serena's sake.

In the morning Juan awakened to the warm blaze of the fire. Don Carlos threw another chunk of wood into the stove and closed its door. Serena had risen, and her blanket lay neatly folded on the floor.

"I did not hear you get up," Juan said getting to his feet.

"Good, good, that is what you needed, sleep. And today you will feel better, no?" Don Carlos said cheerfully. Serena stirred the remains of the corn in the broken pot on top of the stove, while Carlos divided the peaches among them using his knife to spear one for himself.

While they ate, Carlos explained what they must do. "We will take the truck and drive to the orphanage grounds. We will tell the authorities there that you have things to return to the orphans who were so kind to you and your sister. As your uncle I will explain that you are still grieving for your parents and decided to run away and try your luck on your own. You took Serena with you. But I have searched for you and promised to bring you back with me next season. And we go now to Mexico to your grandfather who is waiting for your return."

Juan nodded. He helped Serena fold the other blanket and proceeded to roll them with the flashlight inside. Using another strip from his cloth he tied the roll tightly. He placed the still nearly full jar of syrup in Serena's hands. "You must keep this," he said.

With a last look around, Juan followed Don Carlos and Serena to the truck. The air felt cool and the sun was not shining though they had waited until Carlos was sure the head of the orphanage would be up. It will be a gray day, Juan thought, like his soul.

# THIRTEEN

# Kidnapped!

Wilfred stood looking at the clock in the hall of boys' cottage number three. If he left for school now, he could check to see if the bag behind the rock in the meadow was gone for certain. He pushed his glasses back on his nose and hoisted his books. He preferred knowing to wondering. At the crest of the hill above the old house he stood gazing down. The bag lay where he had left it, but it wasn't that that made him draw in his breath. Pushing back his glasses he stared once more. No mistake, he was looking at a truck parked just off the orchard road. He recognized it as one he had seen back when the migrant workers picked the apples.

Don Carlos might be at the house right now. Had Juan and Serena escaped?

Wilfred ran and didn't stop until he reached Wheelock Cottage. He had to see Jeanmarie, but how? Taking the books from under his arm he knocked on the front door.

111

Leah opened it. "What are you doing here?" she asked. "You delivering something?" She looked around Wilfred as if expecting to see a package of some sort.

"Hi," Wilfred said. "I need to talk to Jeanmarie. It's about a project we've got going." He held up the books for Leah to see.

She stepped back. "Wait here," she said.

Wilfred tried to look bored. When the door opened and Jeanmarie stepped outside, he jumped. "It's important, we need to talk," he said.

"Go around back to the cellar door," Jeanmarie ordered. "I'll get my jacket and we can talk there." Wilfred hurried to the cellar door.

Jeanmarie had her lunch with her when she came. "What is it, Wilfred, another idea?"

"It's Don Carlos. He's back," Wilfred stated. "You can see his truck from the hill."

Jeanmarie felt a surge of fear go through her. "You're sure?" She ran toward the meadow and stopped abruptly. Wilfred was right. The truck below them had to belong to Carlos. She turned to Wilfred. "What will we do? He's come for Juan and Serena. We've got to stop him."

"The only thing we can do now is tell Dr. Werner to call the police," Wilfred said. "I know we promised Juan no police, but it's that or let Carlos kidnap them."

Jeanmarie wanted to do something, stop the man, but Wilfred was right. "Hurry," she said. "We have no time to lose." She let her lunch bag drop and started to run to Dr. Werner's office.

Behind her Wilfred picked up her lunch and ran to catch up.

Dr. Werner looked up as Jeanmarie came bursting into his office and Wilfred after her.

"To what do I owe this entirely unwarranted, undignified, break-in to my office?" Dr. Werner demanded sternly.

"You have to help us," Jeanmarie pleaded. "Someone is about to be kidnapped!"

Dr. Werner's face paled, and he stood to his feet. "What do you mean, kidnapped?"

"Juan and Serena. Don Carlos is down at the migrant workers' house in the orchard right now with his truck. Only he's not their uncle, and he won't let them go home. They ran away, but now he's found them. We have to hurry and do something!" Jeanmarie said breathlessly.

Dr. Werner held up his hand. "Stop at once. What is all this you're telling me? Are you two involved in something? Jeanmarie, be still," he ordered. "Now, Wilfred, you are a boy of intelligence. Tell me what this is all about."

Wilfred started at the beginning, explaining how they had discovered Juan and Serena staying in the old house, Juan's story, and the events following, including the night of the Halloween party. Twice Jeanmarie tried to interrupt, but Dr. Werner sternly silenced her.

Jeanmarie could barely manage to keep still. Every minute counted, and Wilfred was still talking. Silently she pleaded for God to make him stop and make Dr. Werner do something.

"You are absolutely certain of these things, Wilfred?" Dr. Werner asked.

"Yes, sir. Everything."

"You ought to have come to me in the first place," Dr. Werner said, picking up the telephone and dialing. "This is Dr. Werner at the Apple Valley Orphanage; I'd like to report an incident two of our orphans just came to see me about. It appears there is some trouble with one of the Mexican migrant workers and some Mexican children. . . . Yes, that will be fine, Officer Riley. Thank you."

Dr. Werner put down the phone and reached for his coat. "You two come with me."

Jeanmarie glanced at Wilfred as they followed Dr. Werner into the hall and down the steps of the administration building. He was looking straight ahead. Had she done the right thing? Would the police take Juan and Serena to jail? They'd gone for help to save Juan and Serena, but were they too late? "Please, God, don't let it be too late."

Dr. Werner slowed his pace to allow Wilfred and Jeanmarie to keep up. "We should be able to see the migrant workers' house from the top of the girls' hill by the meadow. If they are still there Officer Riley can investigate the matter. It seems to me I recall a dark-haired young man at the Halloween party who spoke with a perfect Spanish accent during one of the games. No doubt it was the boy you call Juan?"

Jeanmarie could barely speak; Dr. Werner *had* heard Juan's slip of the tongue. She managed to say, "Yes, sir, it was Juan. We thought it would cheer them up, I mean the party, sir, and no one would notice them, sir."

"Hmph, so I gather," Dr. Werner said.

Jeanmarie wanted to run and keep running, but Dr. Werner kept walking steadily. Inside she screamed at him to hurry. If only she dared to say it aloud, but she couldn't. She knew she was in enough trouble, Wilfred too.

Behind them the school bell ceased tolling. Dr. Werner said, "You will be late for school of course. I shall give you passes." Jeanmarie had barely noticed the bell, and she wasn't thinking about school.

At the crest of the hill Dr. Werner stood by the meadow fence. "Yes, indeed I do see a truck. And I also see smoke coming from the house chimney. Well, we shall just have to wait until Officer Riley shows up." They waited in silence.

Jeanmarie stared at Wilfred, who did not look at her. He still had her lunch bag and his books under one arm. A few

114

minutes later the sound of a car behind them made her turn. The police!

The officer, an older man with gray hair, stopped his car near them and got out. "Morning, Doctor," he said, extending his hand. "These the two you mentioned? Well now, what seems to be the trouble?"

As Dr. Werner explained to the officer, another sound made Jeanmarie step back in alarm. The truck was coming straight up the road toward them! What was happening? She could see Juan sitting in the small cab and the top of Serena's head next to him. "He has Juan and Serena!" she cried. "Don't let him get away!"

"Easy now, miss," Officer Riley said. "It doesn't look like he wants to get away. I believe he is coming to talk to us."

From the cab of the truck came a loud, cheerful "Buenos dias, señors!" as Carlos stopped next to the police car. He stepped lightly from the truck and touched his wide-brimmed hat in a small salute as he came. Juan and Serena followed. In her arms Serena carried a roll of blankets tied with a strip of white cloth. Jeanmarie recognized the blankets, but why was Juan smiling?

"You have papers?" the officer asked in a friendly manner.

"Sí, Señor Officer, I have the papers." From his pocket he produced papers and handed them to the policeman. "All legal," he said. "We are on our way back to Mexico, no? Only the boy here, he thinks maybe he will stay in the United States and try his luck so he runs away, no? But I have searched everywhere for him and the little one until I found them. I promise him we will return next season to pick the crops." Don Carlos put his hand on Juan's shoulder. "It is very sad, their madre and padre die of the fever in August. We bury them and the children are sad. I think it is why Juan acts so crazy, no?"

The officer handed the papers back to Don Carlos. He drew Juan aside and said kindly, "I am here to help you and your sister if there is something you need. Is this man your uncle as he says?"

"Sí, señor, he is my uncle. I am sorry to cause trouble to others. I will not run away again." He looked at Dr. Werner. "They did not know he is my uncle. They wished only to help my sister and me. I ask their pardon." He did not look at Jeanmarie and Wilfred.

Serena spoke something in Spanish as she placed the roll of blankets in Jeanmarie's arms.

Don Carlos translated. "The little one does not speak the English. She apologizes for her brother's wild stories and for the trouble it caused you. She thanks you for the blankets and the flashlight you loaned them. And she will not forget your kindness or the fine Halloween party."

Dr. Werner shook Don Carlos's hand. "I wish you a safe trip back. I apologize for these two. This one," he tapped Jeanmarie's shoulder, "is too imaginative for her own good. The other should have known better."

Officer Riley smiled and shook Don Carlos's hand. "I have two of my own about their age. I read in the newspaper about the fever outbreak in the workers' camps last August. A mighty shame losing their folks like that." He turned to Juan and Serena. "You mind your uncle and don't go running off. This is a big country."

The officer left and Don Carlos followed with Juan and Serena in the truck. Jeanmarie stood where she was, unable to believe the things she'd heard. Only she knew they must be true. Don Carlos had shown the officer legal papers. Juan admitted he lied. Even Serena! But how could it be? Juan seemed so sincere and Serena so frightened of Don Carlos. Had she mistaken the girl's fears?

Dr. Werner's stern voice roused her. "You and Wilfred will return to my office and wait for me. I have things on my mind. I will come along presently."

Jeanmarie wanted to run, but she walked without looking back. Wilfred kept his pace even with hers. Once Wilfred said in a low voice, "Whatever is on Dr. Werner's mind it has something to do with us. You can bet he's thinking of ways to discipline us."

Jeanmarie glanced over her shoulder to see if Werner was following them. He hadn't moved from the meadow fence. "He's really angry with me," she said. "It doesn't matter. I deserve it for being so dumb." She would never forgive herself or Juan. "Right from the start it was you who doubted Juan's story," she said as Wilfred handed her lunch bag over.

"Maybe I wondered for a little while, but honestly, Jeanmarie, he had me fooled too. Remember, I'm the one who put together all that stuff so he could make a lean-to, and now I'll have to put it all back, that is if Dr. Werner doesn't spot it first." Wilfred looked glum.

"Oh, Wilfred, what have I done to us?" Jeanmarie dreaded whatever was coming, and poor Wilfred really didn't deserve it. "I'm the one who got us into this whole mess," she said, "and Juan with his lies." Why had God let Juan get away with lying like that?

Seated on the hard bench outside Dr. Werner's office, Jeanmarie tried to think of what to say. She couldn't think of a single excuse to use. Wilfred opened a book and read quietly. At the sound of heavy footsteps Jeanmarie's heart began thumping in her chest. She knew whose steps they were.

Inside the office Dr. Werner stood towering above them, his face unsmiling. "You have had time to compose yourselves. I have no doubt you were both deceived by the Mexican boy, but can you tell me why that should excuse your behavior?" Jeanmarie said nothing. Wilfred shook his head. "I thought not," Dr. Werner said. "There is no excuse."

Dr. Werner wrote on a slip of paper from his desk and handed it to Wilfred. Looking directly at him, he said, "You may return to class. I expect you have learned a lesson from your experience, young man. Use your mind, sir. Authorities are for our good use. And until you are head of this orphanage you will obey its rules. Trust must be earned, young man. You are restricted from all off-ground walks for three months, and then we shall see. Regular restrictions from Saturday night affairs will apply for whatever length of time your housemother shall decide. You are dismissed, sir."

Jeanmarie stared at Wilfred. No more of the walks he lived for or romping with the dogs. How would he survive? Wilfred left, closing the door behind him. Jeanmarie felt a chill run down her back as she looked at Dr. Werner.

Dr. Werner walked to the window, then returned to face her, his hands behind his back. "There is a certain streak of stubborn curiosity in you that has been your downfall before now." Jeanmarie knew he meant the trouble she'd had with the FBI. "I see that you do recall the matter," Dr. Werner said, sitting down at his desk.

"Surprising as it may seem to you," he went on, "it is not your curiosity that I am concerned with but how to make you see that you are the one who must control your impulses with good judgment and prudence." Jeanmarie only wished she had some.

Dr. Werner tapped his fingers against the desktop. "Had you come to me I would have listened, and perhaps all that followed would have been avoided." He looked away for a moment and then back at Jeanmarie. "Runaways with no place to go are in grave danger of falling in with those who will exploit them and bring them harm. You would not wish that upon anyone." His voice became stern. "But if your plans to help those two had succeeded it might have brought them only sorrow and trouble in the end. Fortunately, they are safe with their uncle now. But what am I to do with you, young lady?"

Jeanmarie's eyes filled with tears. She truly had meant no harm.

Dr. Werner went on. "You must learn discipline. You will begin by reporting to me once a month on Saturday afternoons at 2:00 sharp, here in my office. You will bring with you a question to discuss. I leave the question to you; my only requirement is it be on a topic of true interest to you." Jeanmarie couldn't believe what she was hearing.

"You too are restricted until further notice from all off-ground activity. Mrs. Ripple will determine the length of restrictions for all activities on orphanage grounds. To be no less than a month, longer as she sees fitting. You will return the blankets, apologize to Mrs. Ripple, and last but not least, I want an essay within two weeks on this whole affair. You are to record all the details in full, including the results. I will be interested in what you have learned, Jeanmarie." He scribbled a note for her return to school. "Dismissed," he said, handing it to her.

Jeanmarie closed the door behind her carefully. How would she survive facing Dr. Werner alone each month? It was the worst part of the punishment. She would probably miss skating this winter at Gould's, and a lot of other things, but nothing compared to this and the essay she was supposed to write. She felt like a criminal who'd just received sentencing for something that wasn't even her fault. She'd be reporting to Dr. Werner like a prisoner to the parole officer.

# FOURTEEN

# Web of Trouble

Jeanmarie stared at the blank paper on her desk, her reading report that should be finished by now. She couldn't concentrate. All day her thoughts kept coming back to the way Juan and his sister had fooled them. Her first shock and disbelief had turned to cold anger. Juan had used her. As for Serena, she could have said anything in Spanish. The two of them probably had had a good laugh at the dumb Americans. When the bell for dismissal rang her paper was still blank.

Pearl stood waiting by the school steps. "I can't believe it," she said. "Juan let us risk our necks for him and his sister and put his uncle through all that too." She touched Jeanmarie's arm. "And you have to take all the punishment," she said softly. "I feel terrible about it."

"Wilfred's hurting too," Jeanmarie said. "I'm glad Dr. Werner doesn't know about you and the others. We were all duped." She brushed a tear of anger from her face. "I don't mind the restrictions so much. But Juan's uncle better never bring him back here. And I hope he pays for all the lies too."

Snowflakes, large wet ones, began to fall by the time Jeanmarie finished her mending work. As she walked home, cold flakes touched her face and landed in perfect little designs on the back of the gloved hand she held out to catch them. For a few minutes she forgot that she still had to face Mrs. Ripple. She shifted the blanket roll under her arm. Mrs. Ripple would never trust her again.

Better to get it over with. Something smelled good as Jeanmarie opened the cellar door. Fresh bread and spaghetti sauce, two of her favorite things. With the blankets still under her arm she went straight upstairs. As Jeanmarie entered the kitchen, Mrs. Ripple was tasting the sauce on the large spoon she held. "I think it's ready," she said, looking up. She laid the spoon on an empty plate and moved to stand by Jeanmarie. "Dr. Werner called. We need to talk, my dear. After supper and chores please come to the sewing room." The sewing room served for both sewing and a kind of office for Mrs. Ripple.

Jeanmarie nodded. She took the blankets upstairs and laid them next to her bed. The keepsake box caught her eye, and anger surged through her. She opened the box and took out her diary. She had plenty to say about liars and people who didn't care how much they hurt others.

She was still writing furiously when Pearl called to her from the doorway. "You okay?" Pearl asked. "It's almost suppertime."

"I'll be there in a minute. I'm almost finished. Done," she said, closing the book and returning it to the box. "Wait a minute; here's something I never want to see again." She held up the carved wooden bird. "I bet he makes them just for dumb Americans like me." She tossed it on her palm. "You can have it if you want it," she said.

"Don't even think it," Pearl said. "I wish we'd never heard of Juan or his bird."

"Maybe he didn't even make it himself," Jeanmarie added. "If he did or not, it makes me furious to think of him at all." The supper bell rang, and she tossed the bird onto the night table where it lay on its side.

In the darkened hallway the lamplight from the sewing room cast a soft, warm glow as Mrs. Ripple opened the door. She had taken off her apron and was wearing a brown gingham dress with white trim at the neck. When she sat down in a large stuffed chair she sat straight and tall. Her face was serious. She motioned Jeanmarie to sit on a nearby stool. She waited silently for Jeanmarie to begin.

Jeanmarie handed her the blanket roll. "I'm sorry I took them. I thought it was to help someone, but it wasn't, not really."

Mrs. Ripple took the blankets, but as she did, the flashlight inside slid partway out. "And the flashlight?" she asked, looking at Jeanmarie.

"Oh no, that's mine. When they gave back the blankets they gave that back too, I guess," Jeanmarie said.

Mrs. Ripple set the flashlight on her sewing table. "You can take it when you go," she said. "I'm confused. Tell me, who did you think you were helping?"

"It's a long story and not a nice one. At least the person we thought needed help wasn't nice. He lied, and he didn't deserve help."

"It sounds like quite a story, Jeanmarie. I'd like to hear it, please."

Jeanmarie began telling her about Juan and Serena, and her part and Wilfred's in the story. "There is so much to tell," Jeanmarie said. "Do you really want to hear it all?"

"All," Mrs. Ripple said.

Jeanmarie twisted her fingers in her lap. When she looked up Mrs. Ripple gently prodded her, "Please go on."

"I promise to tell you everything I did, but I can't name anyone else, please. I just can't."

"You are saying, Jeanmarie, that some of the other girls helped you? I guessed as much. I have noticed some odd behavior lately among you. However, I have no reason to make you reveal the names of anyone. I hope that if others have reason to see me on their own they will. Please continue."

Jeanmarie went on, careful to include everything except the names of any of her friends who'd helped her, other than Wilfred. As she talked her face burned and angry tears came to her eyes. "And that's it. I hate him, and I'll never never forgive him for lying or for what he's brought on Wilfred." Anger overcame her, and with her head in her hands, she wept bitter tears of frustration.

Mrs. Ripple waited for a little while, then handed Jeanmarie a handkerchief. "I'm sure you do feel utterly miserable. And I'm afraid there is no hope that you'll feel any better until you do something about your own sin."

Jeanmarie wiped her face and stared at Mrs. Ripple. "My sin?" she said in a small voice. "Oh. I did sort of tell a lie about the aspirin," she said.

"Yes, and you stole food, coal, matches, blankets," Mrs. Ripple said. "Do you admit that you deceived not only me but your teacher as well? You deceived every time you covered your tracks when you broke the rules, each time you had others cover for you or keep lookout. You were living a lie. And you would have gone on deceiving if Juan's uncle hadn't returned. I wonder how long before all the lies caught up with you."

Jeanmarie tried to look away. Mrs. Ripple's words cut to her heart.

Mrs. Ripple spoke softly. "There was a better way, Jeanmarie, only neither you nor Wilfred took it. Instead you wove a web of trouble for yourself stealing, lying, deceiving, breaking rules, going out at night, and the list could go on. I'm sure the owners of the orchard have no idea how you planned to use their property."

"Oh, please, please," Jeanmarie begged, "I'm so sorry. I never looked at all those things in that way." Sobs choked her. "I should never have listened to that evil boy."

"It is too bad that you can't really be forgiven," Mrs. Ripple stated.

Shocked, Jeanmarie looked at her.

Mrs. Ripple picked up a worn Bible from the table beside her. "I'm sure you know the Lord's Prayer, Jeanmarie," she said. "May I read what Jesus said in Matthew 6:14 and 15, right after he taught that prayer to his disciples?"

Jeanmarie nodded, wondering what Mrs. Ripple meant that she couldn't be forgiven.

Mrs. Ripple read, "If ye forgive men their trespasses, your heavenly Father will also forgive you: but if ye forgive not men their trespasses, neither will your Father forgive your trespasses." She closed the Bible and placed it back on the little table. "I don't see how you can expect to be forgiven for all those trespasses when you refuse to forgive Juan and Serena. Do you?"

"All those trespasses"—the words left a bitter taste in Jeanmarie's mouth. "I lied, I stole, I did all those things too, and

I never thought about it or cared. Breaking rules didn't seem to matter at all as long as I got what I wanted," she said in a small voice. She raised her face and looked at Mrs. Ripple. "If I had come to you and told you about Juan and Serena, what would you have done?"

Mrs. Ripple thought for a moment. "We would have talked, and then I would have prayed for wisdom and guidance, Jeanmarie. Perhaps we could have prayed together, child. After that I don't know. I do know God works in ways we can't even imagine when we bring him our troubles. And even when those ways seem hard to us at the time, or not what we wanted or expected, in the end they will prove to be the best after all. Can you trust him?"

Jeanmarie nodded. "I'm no better than Juan or Serena, and I am sorry for all those things, sorry for lying to you, but I still wish I'd never met Juan."

"You haven't really forgiven him. Is that it?" Mrs. Ripple said gently.

Jeanmarie knew it was true. "Yes," she whispered.

Mrs. Ripple nodded. "We've talked enough for tonight, I think. I don't believe I'll discuss restrictions just now. I'm sure you know there will need to be some."

Jeanmarie picked up the flashlight. "At least a month, Dr. Werner said."

"Well, enough for tonight, child. Run along. We'll talk tomorrow."

Pearl and the others were waiting for her in the dorm. Jeanmarie assured them she'd said nothing about anyone but Wilfred and herself. She didn't say what else they'd talked about. "Go ahead downstairs without me," she begged. "I need to write a letter, take a bath, maybe read."

The letter could wait, and the bath too. She wanted to be by herself for a while.

For a long time she sat on her bed holding the flashlight in her lap. She thought of all that had happened. As she went to put the flashlight on the nightstand, the small wooden carving fell to the floor and rolled under the bed. She bent down to look for it but instead found herself kneeling by her bed thinking. Where were Juan and Serena and their uncle? They would probably drive late into the night before stopping. Serena will need to rest or she'll be sick again, she thought. The night she'd slept with Serena in the cellar flashed through her mind. She remembered Juan's tender look for Serena, who was so sick. The picture of Juan carrying the unconscious Lizzie in his arms came to her mind. Jeanmarie leaned her head against the bed. She didn't really hate Juan, even if he did lie about his uncle. Tears flowed down her face.

Her words were muffled in the bedcovers, but when she finished praying she knew she really had forgiven Juan. "Thanks," she whispered. "I'm glad you made that rule about forgiveness, and I'll let Mrs. Ripple know I'm alright now." She stood up. She'd forgotten all about the little carving. She reached for the flashlight and switched it on to look under the bed.

Something was wrong with the light. Jeanmarie unscrewed the top to check, and pulled out the folded cloth. "How did that get inside?" she muttered. It was a note, one of Juan's sketches. He meant to have her find it all along! She went running from the room to find the others.

Jeanmarie had spread the drawing flat on the floor in front of the others. "That has to be Don Carlos's truck, and these two figures are Juan and Serena."

Maria gasped. "Look! Their mouths are taped and their hands are tied! What does it mean?"

Pearl sat back on her heels. "I think it means that neither of them were free to say anything or do anything but go along with Carlos."

"Then everything Juan told us is true," Jeanmarie said. "Don Carlos must have threatened them somehow to keep them quiet, and the note was Juan's only hope of explaining. No wonder he put the flashlight inside the rolled up blankets."

"But what is that arrow for?" Winnie asked. "It looks like it's pointing to the back of the truck."

"And those little packages with X on them, does that mean X like not good?" Maria said.

Pearl bent closer to the sketch. "I've heard of secret places underneath a truck where things can be hidden, but only in stories. Is that it? Juan is saying look under the truck for something that shouldn't be there!"

"You're right, I know you are," Jeanmarie said. "But what can we do now?"

"Tell Dr. Werner," Winnie said. "Let him do something."

Jeanmarie looked at her. "You're right, Winnie. He should know. Only I don't think he'll believe me. Even if he believes Juan drew the sketch, he can still say it's just a joke or another lie, but I don't think he'll believe me," she said slowly.

"You have to try," Winnie urged. "You can't just let Carlos get away with Juan and Serena and whatever else is in that truck."

"Winnie, I know, and I'll try," Jeanmarie said. "I just don't think he'll believe me now. I've lied and stolen and broken rules, so if he doesn't believe me this time it's my own fault."

"We've all broken rules," Maria said.

"But everything you did was to help Juan and Serena," Pearl insisted in a voice meant to comfort Jeanmarie. "I did those things too," she admitted. "But how can you call it stealing or lying or worry about breaking rules when you have to help someone? You make it all sound so, well, so bad."

"I know," Jeanmarie said. "At the time we thought all those things were okay so long as they worked. But when Mrs. Ripple reminded me of what I'd done, the list sounded the same way to me, bad. She was right. I did do them, only I didn't name them, and I didn't care. Only I do care, because it'll take a miracle to make Werner listen to me now."

Long after lights out Jeanmarie lay awake. In her hand was the little wooden bird. When she finally fell asleep it lay next to her on the pillow.

# FIFTEEN

# A Letter from Mexico

"Dr. Werner isn't in his office right now," the secretary informed Jeanmarie. "He should be back in half an hour. I'll tell him you want to see him." The phone rang and Jeanmarie left.

In her hand she clutched Juan's note. Carefully she placed it inside her notebook. It would have to wait until Dr. Werner came back.

The hallway to the classroom seemed longer than usual, her footsteps heavy. School would start any minute. She knew she should hurry, but she didn't. As she opened the classroom door, Mrs. Gillpin glanced in her direction and frowned slightly.

Mrs. Gillpin announced that a United States Army Intelligence report disclosed that the German Army was three times as strong in the

129

JEANMARIE and the Runaways

field as it was in 1939, and the Luftwaffe Airforce was larger. She read from the *Times:* "'German paratroopers and seaborne invaders have overcome our allied troops on the island of Leros, an important Aegean island. And in the Italian campaign the Germans are entrenched in mountain strongholds from which our troops have not been able to dislodge them as yet.'" Mrs. Gillpin paused. "We must pray for our troops," she said.

Glancing at the paper once more, she smiled. "Now this is an interesting item to lighten our hearts." In a light voice she read the headline: "Rhymed Gibes of Ghost Punctuated Hitler's Speech." Then she read the article to the class. "'A secret radio sender, believed to be located in Poland, broke into Adolf Hitler's Munich speech yesterday with rhymed remarks twitting the Hitler regime and predicting disaster for the German armies in Russia. The ghost voice took advantage of the silence every time Hitler paused for effect, its remarks being clearly heard in Warsaw. The voice repeated rhymed couplets in German time and again, saying: "Let us destroy the Hitler band, then peace again will reach our land. Gone for us in the East our luck, our armies won't return; they're stuck. No more sing Germany Over All; certainly not Hitler's Germany at all."'"

By this time the whole class was laughing. Mrs. Gillpin laid the paper down. "Now I have some truly good news. We have a letter from my friend in Mexico City."

Jeanmarie sat up. She'd forgotten the class letter asking for any information on migrant laborers. Mrs. Gillpin read it aloud, and when she came to one portion of the letter Jeanmarie felt her whole body tense.

"Strange as this may seem," Mrs. Gillpin read, "in light of your class project, recently an old man came to us for help to find his two grandchildren. He had a letter from his grand-

son saying that the boy and his sister were somewhere in New York on their way to pick the apple crop. Apparently the children's parents died in the labor camps, and the children are being exploited by an untrustworthy crew leader. Their grandfather believed the children had also died until a letter from his grandson arrived telling him of their plight. The authorities here say they know nothing, and I fear there is little interest in the grandfather's story. I am thankful for the Mexican children in our orphanage who have been saved from such lives as I fear those two now face. I am sorry for that grandfather and have been praying for him and the children wherever they are. Their names are Serena and Juan."
Jeanmarie heard no more as Mrs. Gillpin continued reading.

Jeanmarie's hands trembled as she smoothed Juan's sketch on her desktop. The moment Mrs. Gillpin assigned the group work for the morning and returned to her desk, Jeanmarie hurried to her. "Oh, Mrs. Gillpin, you won't believe this, but I know those children, Juan and Serena!"

Jeanmarie could feel the tears running down her face as she poured out her heart and showed Juan's sketch.

Mrs. Gillpin's face turned slightly pale as she listened. "God works in mysterious ways," she said finally. "Come, Jeanmarie, this is a matter for Dr. Werner and the police. Class, you will continue working quietly on your projects, and I do mean quietly, until I return. Any disturbance will mean extra assignments for all."

Dr. Werner listened as Mrs. Gillpin explained the sudden visit to his office. His eyes grew wide, then determined, as he picked up the phone and dialed the number of the sheriff's department. "This is Dr. Werner. Sheriff Katz, there's been a kidnapping, and I'm afraid there may also be illegal goods being transported as we speak. . . . Thank you, sir. I'll be waiting."

Jeanmarie felt suddenly drained. Dr. Werner believed her because of Mrs. Gillpin's proof. But had it all come too late?

Dr. Werner thanked Mrs. Gillpin and turned to Jeanmarie. "I shall not excuse you for your activities, but I may reconsider the length of your restrictions as well as Wilfred's under the circumstances. Not that you don't both deserve severe discipline, because you do. But you may have unknowingly done your country a service in stopping an illegal transport of American goods."

Jeanmarie looked at him questioningly.

"No," Dr. Werner said sternly, sensing her unasked question. "You are still to report to me each month as before, Mrs. Ripple's decision on local restrictions will be enforced, and I will expect your essay."

Jeanmarie nodded. Somehow she would get through. It didn't really matter now if only Don Carlos could be stopped.

Dr. Werner sent the school secretary to monitor Mrs. Gillpin's class while the three of them spoke to the sheriff. The sheriff wasted no time in giving orders to his men. "If that truck is anywhere between here and Florida, Carlos won't get away," he assured Dr. Werner. "Thanks to your girl here, we have a good description of the truck and the children as well as Carlos." Jeanmarie felt proud; she knew he meant her.

On the way back to class, Mrs. Gillpin put her arm around Jeanmarie's shoulder. "I know none of these things could have come together by chance. I think the class will have to be told, and I would like you to be the one to tell."

Jeanmarie felt like someone on the way down from the top of a roller coaster as she faced the class. No one made a sound. Mrs. Gillpin smiled and nodded, and Jeanmarie began. "Many of the things I did were wrong, and I know now I should have asked for help. If I had, Juan and Serena might not be in danger, but they are." She told everything, leaving out only the part Pearl, Winnie, and the twins had played. For Wilfred's name she substituted the words *a friend.* Her fear seemed to leave as she talked. At the end she sat down quietly. Hands were raised all over the room, and for several minutes more she answered questions the best she could.

By the time she finished the after-school mending and reached home, the twins had already told Mrs. Ripple the news. She greeted Jeanmarie with a warm hug. "I don't think we need to talk about restrictions just now, dear. There's a certain little girl who needs to know about her 'angel.' You might want to tell her tonight."

"You mean Lizzie?" Jeanmarie had forgotten all about Lizzie seeing Juan. When the last dish was put in place, the coal bucket filled, and the dish towels hung to dry, she went to find Lizzie. "I've something to show you, Lizzie," Jeanmarie said. She led the little girl into the dorm and seated her next to her on the cot.

From the keepsake box she took the carved wooden bird and handed it to Lizzie. "I want to tell you about the boy who made that. His name is Juan." Lizzie's eyes shone with wonder as she listened. When Jeanmarie finished she said, "So, you see, Juan wasn't an angel. Your angel was a real person after all. Of course, that doesn't mean there aren't real angels. It's just that Juan wasn't one of them."

"And yours either," Lizzie said matter of factly.

Jeanmarie raised her eyebrows, puzzled by Lizzie's words. "My angel? What do you mean?"

"You know," Lizzie insisted. "Leah. She's the angel who fills up your coal bucket some mornings so you don't have to. We pretend she's your angel."

Leah had been the one behind the mystery. "It must be because I found her locket," Jeanmarie said slowly.

"Nope," Lizzie said. "She thinks you're nice, but you have a lot on your mind lately, she said."

Jeanmarie kissed Lizzie's forehead. "Thanks. Don't tell her what you told me. It might embarrass her. She is shy, you know. Let's just go on being friendly to her. Okay?"

Lizzie nodded. "Now can I go? May is waiting for me."

Jeanmarie laughed and lifted her down. She watched Lizzie run to the hall. It was a good thing chores changed tomorrow. Poor Leah lugging all that heavy coal by herself.

The wooden bird in Jeanmarie's hand brought her thoughts back to Juan and Serena. She set it on the night table next to the bed to remind her. "I won't forget you wherever you are." Carlos had a whole day's head start. If only Juan could delay his uncle somehow until help came. "Try, Juan, please try," she whispered.

# SIXTEEN

# Surprise
# for Don Carlos

*T*he heater in the old truck worked only on full blast, and
crowded next to Serena, Juan felt hot and cramped. On
the seat something sharp poked at him. His fingers closed
over it, a long metal nail, probably dropped from Don Carlos's tool box. Carefully Juan put it into his pocket. Serena
had fallen asleep, her head leaning toward his shoulder.
Since morning they had driven with only two stops, once at
a rest stop, the next for a flat tire. His throat was dry. He
glanced at Don Carlos.

"We make up for lost time, no?" Carlos said. "If you
had not been so stupid, boy, we would be with the others, no? But no matter, the trees will wait for us."

"What trees?" Juan asked.

"Florida, boy, where the growers must have
workers. Good Mexican workers to pick the
fruit. November, she is the month for the

135

grapefruit and the oranges. December too. My men know where to go. I have arranged all, no? We will unload the truck in Orlando with no one the wiser. Then on to the groves."

Juan's heart sank. Ahead of him and Serena lay the endless days of labor from dawn to dark, day after day. And for what? He shut his eyes. Don Carlos would keep the money, and he and Serena would go on working under him. They would escape again. This time for good.

What seemed like hours passed, and still Carlos drove on. Up ahead Juan saw lights, then gas pumps and a small eating place. Don Carlos yawned and pulled into the empty parking lot.

"Wake up," he ordered, shaking Serena's shoulder. "We make the quick stop here. I will buy food and drinks, no? Go, girl; go with your brother and be quick."

Serena looked about her, bewildered, and Juan took her arm to help her from the truck. He spoke gently to her. Don Carlos strode ahead of them. "Stay in the women's room as long as you can. Trust me," Juan said. He hurried her to the door where Carlos waited. Inside Juan followed Don Carlos to the men's room while Serena entered the women's room.

"Give me the money and I will get a soft drink from the ice chest outside," Juan offered. "I am thirsty."

Carlos counted out the change and handed it to Juan. "Bring two for me," he said.

Juan went quickly to the ice chest and with trembling hands deposited the money in the small metal box attached to it. He removed two bottles and, holding them, ran inside and stood by Carlos who was waiting for his food order. "I will put these in the truck," Juan said. He did not wait for an answer but walked to the door and out. Outside he ran to the truck and threw the bottles on the seat. Quickly he drew the long nail from his pocket and with a smooth rock hammered it into a back tire. The road must do the rest. Juan ran back to the restaurant and sauntered in to wait for Serena. "She is still inside," he said. "I will wait for her."

"Tell her to hurry," Carlos growled. "I do not have all night."

Juan knocked lightly on the door of the women's room, calling Serena's name. She came out looking puzzled but said nothing. The three piled back into the truck and pulled onto the road. Juan had just unwrapped his hot dog when the truck began to bump and thump and swerve. Carlos cursed, pulled off the road, and got out. A string of loud complaints followed. Juan climbed down to see the damage.

"Two flats in one night. She is a devil, this truck. Help me, boy," Carlos said. "The spare is no good. I will take off the tire. You must go back up the road with it to the air pump. We will need the patches from the truck to fix it. You know how to fix it, no?" Juan nodded. He had helped Carlos before with flat tires when his padre was still alive.

It grew colder and very late by the time they were done. Juan climbed wearily into the truck. His arms were heavy, his eyes ready to close. Serena was sound asleep. Don Carlos slammed the door on his side and started the truck. Sometime in the middle of the night the truck stopped. Carlos had pulled off the road into a small rest area. "We will sleep here a while," he said. "We lost much time, but we will make it up. The tires are fixed, and the truck, she behaves, no? Stay with your sister until I come back. If she wakes, I do not want her to be frightened." Carlos left the truck and disappeared down the path to the deserted outhouses.

To himself Juan said, It is you who frighten her. This was the moment he had waited for. He had no nails left, but he would not need nails this time. Quietly he picked up the jar of syrup Jeanmarie had given Serena, then he opened the door and slid to the ground. The gas cap was on this side of the truck. Quickly he unscrewed the lid from the jar of syrup in his hand. Holding his breath he undid the gas cap and emptied the syrup into the tank. He threw the empty jar into the grass. His hands trembled as he fastened the gas cap. With the cap back in place he moved back to the door of the truck, stood against it, and stretched. After a few minutes Carlos returned and signaled Juan that it was his turn.

They left at daybreak. Before they reached the next town the truck motor began to make a new sound, and then nothing. The truck would not go. Carlos got out and looked under the hood. "Start her when I give the word," he ordered Juan. "Now!" Carlos said. "Did you hear, boy, start her now!" he commanded. Nothing happened. "Move over, boy, I will do it myself," he roared. The truck did nothing. Carlos got out and kicked its side savagely. "Come," he ordered Juan, "we will push her. Your sister will steer."

A bright sun shone in the November sky, and the cool breeze felt good as Juan pushed alongside Carlos. "Ay caramba," Carlos panted. "She is a devil, this one."

"The devil is not your truck," Juan murmured, too softly for Carlos to hear.

When they finally arrived at a gas station, the man who looked under the hood seemed puzzled. All day, between customers, he worked on the truck with Carlos alongside. The ancient truck had many parts that long ago needed replacing, but each one the mechanic pointed out brought a groan from Carlos and insistence it could not be the fault. Late in the afternoon the man decided something was wrong with the gas tank system. It was full of a sticky substance. "No wonder she don't run. Looks like somebody's dumped sugar syrup into her," the man said.

Juan backed away, ready to run, as Carlos came toward him with his arm raised. At that very moment a police car pulled into the station. Carlos lowered his fist as he said, "Later you will pay."

Two state patrol officers stepped from the car, hands on their guns. "Put your hands on your head and stand next to the truck," one of them said.

"Señor Officer, I have papers. My children and I, we do nothing wrong. It is some mistake, no?" Don Carlos's eyes grew wary as the other officer tapped the wooden platform in back of the truck. "I think we're onto something here," he called to his partner.

The officer made Juan and Serena stand by while he handcuffed Don Carlos and placed him in the back of the police car. "You must be the children we're looking for," he said.

"I am Juan; this is my sister, Serena. The man in your car is Don Carlos. He is an evil man and a liar, and he is not our uncle."

"That's what we've been told," the policeman said. "Lucky for you two we happened along when we did." Juan nodded. "You'll be okay now," he said, patting Serena's head.

"She does not understand the English," Juan said, "but she knows you have captured Don Carlos, and she is happy."

"Tell her she has good reason to be happy. It looks like someone back in New York started an all out search for you and that truck of contraband. You two will be going home in style."

Juan grinned. He was tired and dirty and hungry, but his heart was full.

Monday morning it snowed. Jeanmarie watched it from the upstairs hall window. From here the old house looked picturesque, its roof covered with white. The field blanketed in white and the fence topped with snow made a beautiful picture, and it would stay that way undisturbed by anyone the rest of the winter. She wished Juan and Serena could have seen it this way.

At school mild chaos reigned inside the classroom where Mrs. Gillpin had not yet arrived. The sudden opening and shutting of a door brought complete silence. "I see," Mrs. Gillpin said, "that you did not take advantage of this extra time to do something constructive. I am disappointed." Mrs. Gillpin's face, rosy from the cold, looked stern. "Take out your notebooks and pencils. Let's see how well you do on a little spelling test." It wasn't like Mrs. Gillpin to spring a test like this. Jeanmarie looked at Pearl, who shrugged her shoulders and took out her notebook.

"First word—*Juan*," Mrs. Gillpin said. "Don't look so surprised. I expect you to know something besides the words in your spellers. Second word—*Serena*." Jeanmarie liked the way Serena looked on the page. She lifted her pencil ready for the next one. *"Found,"* said Mrs. Gillpin and smiled. For a second Jeanmarie almost wrote the word, then the class began cheering. Hands went up, Jeanmarie's among them.

"Let me tell you what I know," Mrs. Gillpin told them. "Juan and Serena are safe and on their way home to Mexico. Dr. Werner made many phone calls on their behalf, and I made one myself to my missionary friend in the orphanage. The children will stay there once they arrive until arrangements can be made to contact their grandfather." Jeanmarie could have hugged her.

"Now, class, I have some other news I think you will like also." Mrs. Gillpin tapped her desk for attention. "With Dr. Werner's backing, we have received permission from the owners of Benson's Apple Orchard for a class project."

"Picking apples next year?" one of the boys called out.

"No, nothing like that," Mrs. Gillpin said. "If you are willing, class, as soon as the weather permits in spring, we may see what we can do to fix up the migrant workers' place in the orchard. Next year's migrants will come to a clean, repaired house, with curtains on the windows and whatever else we can do to make them welcome."

Jeanmarie had a faraway look on her face. She touched the small wooden bird hanging from a ribbon around her neck. Wilfred pushed his glasses back on his nose. "Just about spring I'll be off restrictions, so no more grand ideas please," he warned.

Jeanmarie smiled.

# More about This Book

The author once lived in an orphanage like the one in the Jeanmarie books and saw migrant workers harvesting the apples in a nearby orchard. The house provided for the workers by the orchard owners was old and in great need of repairs. Their labor was greatly needed because so many farm workers had gone off to the war.

Migrant workers have been coming to our country to help harvest crops ever since World War II. Some of them come legally, but many who are willing to work for little pay under poor conditions and are desperate for work make their way into the United States illegally. Life for the workers and their families is often a hard one, especially for the children, as they move about following the crops.

Even today some migrant farm workers are forced to sleep in cars, at campsites, or in very poor housing. Sadly, housing for the migrants is little better than it was years ago.

Migrant farm families suffer more diseases and have more accidents than other workers. Many migrants still must deal with dishonest growers and crew leaders. The government has passed some laws to help them, and we now have rules meant to protect the workers from pesticides and fines for health violations in migrant labor camps. But much more help is needed to see that the laws are enforced and that others are passed.

During World War II the help of Mexican laborers called *braceros* saved the crops in the United States. Migrant workers are still an important part of American farming, and new groups of workers continue to come north each year to the States hoping for work. Children like Juan and Serena still toil in the fields alongside their parents.

# Spanish Words Used in the Story

| | |
|---|---|
| *ay caramba* | a slang expression of surprise |
| *braceros* | Mexican migrant laborers during World War II who came under an agreement with the Mexican government |
| *buenos dias* | good day |
| *gracias* | thank you |
| *madre* | mother |
| *muerte* | dead |
| *padre* | father |
| *por favor* | please |
| *señorita* | Miss |
| *señor* | Mr. |
| *sí* | yes |
| *Vaya con Dios* | go with God |